LEXI GREENE

Desert Prince, Scandalous Affair

First published by Warrior Heart Publishing 2018

Copyright © 2018 by Lexi Greene

This novel is entirely a work of fiction. The names, characters and incidents portrayed in it are the work of the author's imagination. Any resemblance to actual persons, living or dead, events or localities is entirely coincidental.

Lexi Greene asserts the moral right to be identified as the author of this work.

First edition

ISBN: 978-0-6483874-2-8

This book was professionally typeset on Reedsy.
Find out more at reedsy.com

Acknowledgement

A big thank you to my editor Jena O'Connor, my proofreader Janice Owen, and to the gorgeous Joanne Dannon, Beverley Eikli and Nina Campbell for believing in me and keeping me on track. Thank you to Romance Writers of Australia and Romance Writers of America, and to Margie Lawson for making my writing better.

Acknowledgements

Chapter One

Macadamia nut ice cream was better than sex.

Jemma savoured the slide of the spoon over her tongue. The sun had just reached its zenith and a balmy breeze whispered through her number-five, honey-blonde hair. She sat at a small table outside Kerb's Boathouse in Central Park. A model yacht angled through the water with a soft, silky splash and trees gave benevolent shade, their leafy limbs stretching high in what was an urban oasis. Her eyes closed and she relaxed fully for the first time in... forever. With the sun warming her skin and ice cream storming her senses, she was as close to happy as she'd ever been.

Her phone rang and the musical tone was magic to her ears. Aminah's name flashed on the screen. At last. Her blood raced with a top-shelf happy buzz. She snatched up her mobile, swiping the stickiness from her lips. "Hello!"

A deep, dark, gravelly voice barked at her. "Who are you?"

Jemma sat upright with a rush of adrenaline. "Who are *you*?" She struggled to draw breath against the tight band that squeezed her chest. She couldn't breathe. She couldn't move. Something was wrong. Had someone learned of their plans to get Aminah away from her brother and out of Zahidah?

"I asked you first."

His tone was a low-pitched growl and flint to her red-headed temper. "I'm not in the habit of divulging personal information to a stranger. Call it self-preservation." The summer sun, so pleasant moments before, now seemed to scorch right through to her bones.

"And I'm not in the habit of allowing others to defy me. Why is your number the only number on my sister's mobile phone? A phone I wasn't aware she owned."

His sister?

Prince Rashid bin Ra'ed Al Shahid? The reigning prince of Zahidah?

Oh crap, oh crap. The Earth stopped spinning and the birds fell silent. Time ceased. Nothing existed except for the harsh intake of breath on the other end of the line. Jemma's stomach churned. She hadn't spoken to this man—the father of her child—in five years. Five years since she lost her sanity in the arms of a stranger. One crazy night. One crazy lie. Secrets lay between them like a minefield. "Where's Aminah?"

"Answer my question. Your number is the only number in the log of this phone, and it appears with prolific regularity. Why is that?"

His English was perfect for a man whose first language was Zahidan. She was the one who grappled for words. So many, but so few of them were safe.

"Who. Are. You?" Each word was a sharp-edged thrust.

"A friend of Aminah's." Jemma's bravado sounded wafer-thin. How had he come to have Aminah's phone? She leapt to her feet. If he so ordained, his henchmen from the Zahidan embassy in New York could be by her side in less time than it took her to dump her unwanted treat in a nearby bin. *Sami.* An invisible fist tightened around her throat. Her blood

2

rushed—gushed—in her ears. Her pulse throbbed. This wasn't about Sami. This was about Aminah. But Sami was his too and Jemma had been in the grip of panic since she'd learned who the father of her child truly was.

"*Princess* Aminah."

Could his tone be any haughtier? Where was the dark, handsome cliché she'd met in a Sydney bar who'd lured her into his arms with his humour and warmth? Who'd swept her off her feet and taken her to heaven? "I'd like to speak with her. Please."

"Princess Aminah is indisposed." His tone was carefully neutral.

"Indisposed how?" Jemma's heels banged against the concrete path as she paced. The tall buildings at the verge of the park seemed to lurch towards her like gnashing teeth. Had he discovered the truth? Had he discovered their plans? The questions tied her in knots and left her witless.

"Perhaps you'd like to meet with me and discuss it further," he said with an authority that left her in no doubt as to the answer he expected.

"No," she choked out. "Thank you. I'm not able to meet with you. Could you please ask Aminah—*Princess* Aminah—to call me at her earliest convenience?" An I-will-fight-you-to-the-death determination filled her bones with steel. Their tell-all book would be a *New York Times* Bestseller and soon the whole world would know what kind of man the King of Zahidah really was.

No wonder the queen sought solace in the arms of another man all those years ago.

The custom of arranged marriages was alive and well in Zahidah. No young woman should be forced by her father—or her brother—to marry a man three times her age. Aminah's farce of a marriage could not go ahead. Jemma might share a daughter with the man on the other end of the phone, but that didn't mean she had to like him.

"Princess Aminah disappeared last night. She was taken by force." Stark, furious, and rattle-snake quick, his words were desert-dry and bereft of compassion.

Jemma felt every one of them like a lash. Aminah was in danger? Or so he wanted her to believe. She didn't trust him. Not when he wanted Aminah to marry against her will. Not when Aminah had asked Jemma for help. "I don't believe you."

"Then I'll ask her to return your call at her earliest convenience. Who shall I direct her to call?"

"Jemma."

"Jemma who?"

"Just Jemma. She knows who I am." Unlike the father of her child who thankfully didn't recognise her voice. Why would he? It was one night, and she'd lied to keep it that way. She didn't like anyone to get close and this man? This man had touched the sad, lonely child inside of her—deeply—in a way that left scars. So, they'd connected. It wasn't like they'd fallen in love. It was a night of wild lust. A night of abandon. A night of soul-deep connection that created a gift of life. Sami. A gift she treasured over any other.

"I'll pass on the message, 'Just Jemma.' Of course, you may have a long wait."

Jemma's legs buckled beneath her and she sank down onto the hard, concrete path. She took a deep breath. Aminah was fine. She had to be. Toughen up, Jemma. Get it together. He's a bully, just like his father.

"If you are responsible in any way for her disappearance," he said, pausing to emphasise the threat, "you'll pay."

"I'm not responsible, but I'll take my chances." There was no sign of gut-roiling emotion on his side of the phone.

"Good luck with those."

Jemma jabbed at the keypad and terminated the connection. The world around her came back into livid focus. Over *her* dead body. The last thing she would do was accept *Prince* Rashid's version of the truth. His head was so far buried in the sand, he wouldn't know the truth if it smacked him.

She struggled to her feet and wobbled as she regained her balance. The paths that earlier had seemed so well marked became a labyrinth. The sun beat down on her. The concrete beneath her sandals was molten and sticky with heat. Every step was laboured, and her clothing pressed on her lungs. She couldn't think. She needed to speak with Aminah. Aminah would tell her it was all a crazy mistake.

The trees, the sky, the paths swirled in front of her eyes. She cupped her hands around her mouth and nose, and gradually—slowly—the sun-scorched air stopped catching in her throat, her heartbeat eased from a frenzied gallop to a run, from a run to a laboured limp. She collapsed onto a bench and the relief was a revelation as if her feet hadn't known not-walking was an option.

It will be okay. I will find Aminah and I will set her free.

Free to marry whomever she pleased. Free to make the mistake of a one-night stand. She shook the thought from her mind. Sami was the best thing that had happened in her life. Closely followed by Aminah. She wished Sami was in New York and not back in Zahidah with Margie. It was the first time she'd travelled without them, but she'd decided the disruption to Sami's routine wasn't worth it. Not when her recovery from the bone marrow transplant was going so well.

Fear was like an icy breeze over her heated skin. Sami was okay. Sami was fine. Rashid didn't even know she existed. Sami was safe. But Aminah? What if Prince Rashid moved the wedding forward? What if Aminah had done as she'd threatened and taken her own life? Jemma clenched her jaw. No. Aminah had promised to let Jemma fix this and fix it she would.

"Just Jemma." Rashid's fury clenched in his stomach like a fist. No woman had ever spoken to him with such disrespect. To imply he was lying or spinning a falsehood about the very real, very awful events unfolding around him was cruelty in the extreme. The police station in Zahidah's capital was lit with bare bulbs and the glare pinched his sleep-deprived eyes. His gaze dropped to the counter and the plastic bag which held his sister's belongings, abandoned when she was forced into a vehicle. Her handbag was damaged, but the phone had survived intact. A mobile phone? Between the ache in his heart for Aminah, his fear for her life, and the anger that razed him from the inside out, he couldn't think. Too much had happened in too short a space of time.

His father waited.

He slipped the phone into the folds of his *thawb*.

Who'd given it to her? This woman? Jemma? The screen background showed a photo of two women, their faces veiled. One set of eyes a stunning emerald green, bewitching, like something out of a Western fairy tale. The other, dark, dark brown like a doe's. They both looked bright, happy and joyous. Emotions he hadn't seen in Aminah's eyes for a very long time, if ever. It was the kind of photo young women take, the camera held at arm's length, their two faces beaming, half chopped, close together. Jemma had earned Aminah's trust it seemed.

Aminah had been out in the Zahidan capital at night—alone and unprotected. His security staff hadn't kept her safe. *He* hadn't kept her safe. The thought clawed at him. It tore and gouged his heart. What if his enemies had taken her? Killed her? No. He refused to believe it. Aminah was a princess. A member of the royal family. More likely, they'd receive a ransom demand. Maybe it had something to do with this woman. Jemma. Had she befriended his sister with malice in mind? Aminah could be dead. He took a deep breath and exhaled slowly. He should have curtailed her freedom. He should have refused her the many hours she volunteered at the children's hospital.

Rashid scrunched the top of the plastic bag with sweaty hands and steeled himself to thank the police officer, accepting the sympathy in his eyes. Rashid would find Aminah and those responsible would pay. He pushed through the door and strode back along the corridor with its clean linoleum flooring.

"Father, we're done here. Let's get you back to the palace." He helped the elderly man to his feet. His father struggled to walk these days. "Are you okay?"

His father nodded, the frailty of his body belying the strength of his spirit. "How did Aminah come to be out in the city—alone—at night?"

His puzzlement scraped at Rashid's frayed nerve endings. How *had* Aminah come to be out at night? He shortened his steps to suit his father's and they left the cool comfort of the building to face the crowd of photographers and journalists with microphones and TV cameras who jostled for news. The sun had barely begun its blistering arc, yet its rays seared like a soldering iron. A black limousine waited a short distance from the door. Rashid schooled his expression carefully as he fought for calm. "There is no news yet. I apologise," he said, with kind deference to their concern. "Thank you for your care."

Rashid didn't answer his father's question until the door closed with a sharp thud and they were in private space, a glass shield between them and the driver. "I, too, would like to know why Aminah was not better protected. It's a question for our head of security." His heart pounded like a fist inside his chest, and every breath knotted and caught in his throat.

"Your mother has taken to her rooms and the women are visiting her there," his father said with a short, wheezy breath. "How could Aminah be so careless and irresponsible?"

The brief exercise had taxed him. It was a reminder of how frail he'd become in recent years. "You blame Aminah?" His father's lack of warmth towards his sister was a constant source of discomfort. "My security staff failed *her*. Not the other way around." *He* had failed her. Guilt poked Rashid, but he poked it right back. The fault lay with those who had perpetrated the crime; with royal life which made her a target in the first place. "You've always expected so much of her."

"And I've always been disappointed."

"This was hardly her fault." Rashid tasted the familiar bitterness. He was the first son and worthy of respect, but his sister had done nothing to deserve his father's disregard.

"Our people need strong leadership and reassurance in this unstable time. I have reassured Sheikh Kamil that Aminah will be found and the wedding will go ahead."

Rashid sat rigid, his sister's belongings in a plastic bag on his knee. His sister's disappearance had left an uncomfortable void in his life and for the first time, he saw clearly what he'd refused to see. His father was largely indifferent towards her. He'd assumed it was because she was a woman in a man's world, but now he saw the unadulterated truth. His father was displeased and inconvenienced by Aminah's disappearance, but his behaviour was far from that of a loving father who feared for the life of his daughter.

Rashid thought back to his last meeting with Aminah. She'd begged him to reconsider her marriage to Kamil. Her dark eyes had sparkled with tears, her cheeks had flushed, her lips were bruised pink from her teeth. Beautiful, but as flighty as Sha'hir, his favourite mare. He'd soothed and reassured her but had insisted the marriage must go ahead. It was important. Frustration tied him in knots.

"You must find Aminah and deliver her to Kamil. Leave no stone unturned and the perpetrator's punishment must be public and severe."

"Kamil is the least of my worries." Never had he openly defied his father, but unlike Aminah, he'd been brought up to believe in the value of his own opinion. "Aminah's life is at stake, her well-being." Rashid would find her if it was the last thing he did. Just Jemma's voice was etched into his mind. She had to be involved in Aminah's disappearance. Aminah's behaviour had changed. Never had she argued with him before, her eyes ablaze with defiance. No doubt encouraged by this so-called friend. A promise formed in the fiery stuff that pounded in his temple. He would find answers from this woman and he would seek justice. If she'd had even a small part in this fiasco, she would pay.

"Zahidah is at risk. Its people are at risk." His father's words were like waves on the shore; a percussive monologue he'd heard his entire life. "Nothing is as important as Aminah's wedding."

"Not even her life?"

"This marriage is vital, and you know it."

Rashid was well aware of his father's machinations. His thoughts shifted to his own betrothal with Kamil's daughter, Fadila. The mere thought of her was enough to ravage his pride. He'd failed in his duty. He'd failed to reclaim the lost lands of Zahidah. His promise to his grandfather sat heavily in his gut. The land and what was hidden beneath it were vital to Zahidah's future. There was no choice. Aminah must pay for his failure. There was no other way.

God knew he'd kept his promise to marry Fadila when every cell in his body had hungered for another woman. A woman he'd known for one night. A woman whose hair was the colour of the sunset over the desert… more fool him. Women were fickle at best and deceitful at worst.

The arrangement was in Aminah's best interest. It was a win-win. Besides, her final acceptance of his argument had led him to believe she understood the importance of her betrothal. This was no more than it seemed. Aminah's captors would make their move and when they did, he'd be waiting.

Rashid watched the sandstone buildings fall away as the long, sleek vehicle moved through the streets. Women were draped in black, their faces veiled, their movements slow, as if they too were shell-shocked by what had happened. Even the tourists seemed conscious of the sombre air. Their princess was missing. Abducted. News travelled fast.

His chest heaved as he fought to draw breath into his strangled lungs.

With ten years between them, he remembered when Aminah

was born, her first words, her first steps. But he'd been absent for much of her youth, attending a Western boarding school. Holidays had been further schooling in his home country and in his own language.

When the car drew up in front of the sprawling palace, he didn't wait for his father to leave the vehicle first. Nor did he wait for Makeen to open his door. Surprised, the older man stepped back, his head bowed, his condolences soft on the heated air.

"Thank you, Makeen. We *will* find her." *I* will find her. His father's lack of concern for Aminah's well-being brought a new twist to the blade that tormented his gut. He couldn't equate the man he'd loved and respected his entire life with the bitter, cold-hearted words that had spilled from his lips. Why wasn't his father beside himself with worry? Did he care so little? The thought sickened him or perhaps it was his own fear for Aminah's well-being that had bile in his throat. He forced himself to assist the older man. His father laboured over every step, air whistling from his lungs. Compassion for his father fought with steely anger and he struggled to keep his expression from betraying the depths of it. Honour and commitment to his country were as integral to him as his bones. He'd learned from his youngest years about priority and responsibility. But what of family? Should Zahidah's lost lands take precedence over his sister's well-being?

After settling his father to rest and arranging a cold drink for his refreshment, Rashid traversed the vast hall, his heels loud against the mosaic tiles, his mind oblivious to the opulence of his surroundings. He strode with long steps towards the stateroom where his security staff worked with the Zahidan police.

He fingered the phone secreted in the folds of his robes.

Soon he would know what form of devilry had played out between his sister and the woman she'd befriended. Soon he would have answers to the questions that ravaged his mind.

Jemma was key. A woman who'd filled his sister's head with nonsense about female liberation and look where it had gotten her. Into his enemies' hands. Had they somehow learned of the vast reserves of oil that lay like an Aladdin's cave beneath the water-rich lands stolen by the Daiji? But how was it possible? Not even his father knew of the freshly signed oil deal he'd negotiated with a consortium from the West. But to deliver on his promise, he needed the land. It would guarantee Zahidah's prosperity for this generation and many to come. The land was beyond important. Rich with water, rich with oil. It was the jewel in Zahidah's crown and if his enemies were to learn of its true riches? It would be lost to his people forever. Jemma was the only clue to what had transpired, and he was determined to find her. He would find her and when he did, she'd wish he hadn't.

Chapter Two

" I 'm sorry, Jemma. This must be heartbreaking for you."
There was sympathy in Nola's gaze. They were seated at
a small café around the corner from the stylist who was
about to work her magic and make them both gorgeous and
glamorous for Nola's wedding ceremony that evening. Nola
wasn't the type for a princess dress or church wedding and nor
was her partner, Brad. The rooftop of their favourite nightclub
was more their scene and the weather was perfect for it.

Jemma hoped the makeup artist could hide the effects of too
little sleep. She held Nola's gaze over the rim of her cup, the
scent of the rich, freshly brewed coffee doing little to soothe
the fire that raged in her veins. "That royal pain of a man
spoke to me like I was the one who forced Aminah into some
god-forsaken corner. She could be dead or held captive by
lunatics or worse. This is his fault." The words were bitter
on her tongue and she washed them away with a deep gulp of
coffee, the liquid burning all the way to her stomach.

Nola's gaze held hers over the modern, tortoise-shell rimmed
glasses that balanced on the end of her nose. Jemma was in
New York for Nola's wedding and a bride needed her maid of
honour, even if party-mode seemed like an alternate universe
and Jemma had to fight every instinct to jump on the next flight

home. This was a once in a lifetime celebration for Nola and no way would she let her editor and long-time friend down. She had to pull herself together and smile.

"Aminah is a princess," Nola reflected. "She's worth more alive than dead. Rashid's security people will be all over this."

"You're right. I just hate feeling powerless." Jemma rummaged in her bag and withdrew a tissue. "You must be looking forward to your trip to Bora Bora. I can't wait to see your photos. The villas over the water look spectacular. Imagine sleeping with the sound of the water lapping beneath you."

"I am looking forward to it, but I'm not planning on sleeping," Nola said with a grin. "St. Regis looks too good to miss a moment."

"And I'm guessing your not-sleeping would have nothing to do with your gorgeous hubby-to-be?"

"Nothing." The sparkle in Nola's eyes belied her words. "What did you think of your cover art?"

"I loved it." The title stood out in bold, metallic pink lettering over a closely cropped picture of Aminah, her face veiled, her black, thickly lashed eyes, so hauntingly beautiful, so achingly sad. Tears blurred Jemma's vision. She fought them back and lowered her cup to the table. "It looks amazing."

"It does." Nola wrapped her arm around Jemma and squeezed her in a compassionate hug. "The book will be an outstanding success. Another bestseller. Aminah will be found and when she is, you can celebrate together. If she was forced to marry against her will, her story will be publicised far and wide, and Kamil will know the truth. He'll feel duped and annul the arrangement. Your plan is genius. Now, it's time to go. There's glamming-up to be done."

"Thanks, Nola. For everything…"

Nola released her and the freeze-frame in Jemma's body eased. She wasn't a touchy-feely kind of person, unlike Nola, who ran on high-octane fuel, energy zapping in the air around her. Nola reached for her mandarin orange bag and took one last swig of her latte. She lowered the empty cup and said, "I'm going to the bathroom. It'll be okay. Aminah will be found and all will be well."

Jemma eyed her friend through watery vision and tried to smile. "Yes, you're right."

"You've done a brilliant job with the book. Aminah's story is compelling and will create a wave of compassion for the women of Zahidah and other countries like it. Aminah will be thrilled with the book. It's a credit to you both."

Jemma nodded. The words she needed just wouldn't come.

"You look good in glasses, by the way."

"Thanks." She'd taken to wearing coloured contacts in Zahidah. With Zahidah's tradition of women covering their faces with a veil, her eyes were the only thing that could give her away. She'd been careful. Very careful.

Nola nodded. With a flash of colour and overpowering perfume, she disappeared towards the Ladies. Jemma's very own fairy godmother, but not even Nola could bring Aminah back. Jemma sat in front of her barely touched coffee. Aminah's story would be told and Nola was right. Aminah would be found and all would be well.

Jemma forced oxygen into her lungs. She could do this. She would follow the plan she and Aminah had worked out together. The book was pivotal. The neighbouring sheikh would refuse to marry Aminah when he learned she was half-royal and half-who knew what. The palace security services would find Aminah—*if* they hadn't been involved in her kidnapping in the first place. Jemma just had to wait and hope they'd find Aminah, alive and untouched. She refused to consider any other alternative. Worse, she had to hope the palace would not find the passport she and Aminah had organised for her departure.

They'd been so close to leaving... Jemma wanted to howl her frustration. Had their plans been discovered? Had the king secured Aminah until the wedding in four weeks' time? Or had Aminah followed through with her threat to take her own life? Jemma pushed the abhorrent thought away. It opened wounds not yet healed. Memories of her father and what he had done. She needed the solid reality of the book in her hands; everything else was shifting sand.

Jemma pushed herself off the stool and waited while her legs wobbled and strained to find strength. The book had been accepted for publication. The contract was signed. The release date was pending. She couldn't stop it. Not now. It wasn't possible. It was like a runaway camel with a knife in its belly. But, with Aminah missing, her plan had unravelled.

The door to Jemma's rented apartment slammed behind her on a gust of wind and Jemma jumped. Her insides twisted. A wave of emotion constricted her throat, too familiar, too much a part of her earliest memories. Fear. She rejected it and straightened her spine. No crying. She wouldn't mess up her face, not after the hours the make-up artist had spent perfecting it. She had to stay focused. Change into her dress. Get to the ceremony on time. Help Nola and Brad make their vows to love each other for the rest of their lives. How different this wedding would be from the one Aminah feared. Nola had looked happy and excited, glamorous and gorgeous, her blonde hair edgy and flattering. No tears. No fears. So much hope and positivity. If only Nola's energy could be bottled and taken medicinally.

Jemma glanced at her watch. She had half an hour to get ready and with the time difference, she'd have time to call Sami.

"Hi, Margie. Is Sami there?"

"Sure is. Give me a moment. We've been icing cupcakes."

"Sounds like fun."

"Here she is."

Jemma's heart swelled and her throat tightened. She wouldn't cry. She forced happy into her tone. "Hi, precious honey. How's it going?"

"Good."

"How are you feeling?" Sami's health had been her focus for so long, the question was out before she'd thought better of it.

"Good."

"I miss you. I love you to the moon and the sun and the stars."

"I love you to the moon and the sun and the stars, and back again."

Sami's words brought a smile to her face. "I love you more than I can say. Always."

"When are you coming home?" Sami's tone was excited.

"Tomorrow, and I can't wait to see you, but I have to go now."

"Okay, Mummy."

"Bye, my darling. I miss you already." Jemma's heart twisted in her chest and the ache lodged there. She hated being away from Sami. The silence in the apartment was heavy and sucked at her energy.

As a child, her life had always felt unstable, uncertain and scary. Her father's relentless travel and fluctuating depression hadn't helped. Her chest cramped with love and grief and even

17

now, her loss seemed as raw and sharp-edged as the day he'd passed. She didn't want that kind of childhood for Sami. She wanted Sami to be well and to feel safe. She wanted Sami to live a carefree, happy life. Instead, her tiny daughter had battled leukemia and knew nothing of her father.

Jemma positioned cobalt-coloured contact lenses over her naturally turquoise eyes, touched up her lips with a soft rosy hue and slipped into a breezy blue dress. Smoothing it over her hips, she stepped into neutral coloured heels and reached for a matching handbag. She texted Nola. *On my way. How are you feeling?*

An answering text pinged into her phone before she'd hit the bottom of the stairs and pushed out into the balmy night air: *Can't wait. See you at the Red Hummingbird.*

Jemma pushed her long, unruly, refused-to-be-tamed, golden—thanks to hair colour because a girl can't be too careful—strands of hair back from her face and took a deep breath. The spices, garlic, and restaurant smells brought hunger to her stomach. She needed to eat. Food hadn't been high on her list of priorities. The streets were busy, a bustle of evening crowds, taxis, and honking vehicles. Funny how she felt even more alone when surrounded by others. It was a loneliness that hurt. More so tonight. She couldn't wait to get back to Sami. And Margie. And Aminah. They were family. Her family.

Rashid looked up at the narrow stone building, squeezed between two marble-fronted, multi-level high rises.

New York was light years from Zahidah.

He spoke into his smartphone. "The Red Hummingbird? You're sure?" He ended the call with a sharp thank you. He had the element of surprise and it looked like his girl was out partying. Jemma's mobile phone was a most helpful GPS device. Why weren't young women more aware of the dangers of the location services on their phone? Not to mention those connected with their camera. Men of a sinister mind could not only access their photos but could locate them in real time. Too easy. Burglars, stalkers, even princes could use that information to their advantage.

Not that Jemma was foolish enough to advertise her home address on her social networking page. Hence, the reason he was here. It was better than ruining the carpet in his penthouse with his furious pacing. He was too wound up to wait until morning. Besides, this was the perfect opportunity to catch her off guard. If this was the kind of woman his sister colluded with, he held grave fears.

Why had Jemma sought Aminah out? What did she hope to gain? In his experience, it was always about personal gain. It was human nature to want more. Had she been paid off by Aminah's abductors? Had she taken Aminah herself? Was Aminah here, in New York, partying in a bar?

It was a long while since he'd frequented a Western nightclub and he was shocked by the throb of sexual energy, the loud music, and the thick air. He spied the bar over the top of the gyrating, overheated, barely clad bodies and saw it as a haven of sorts. He scanned the crowd for Jemma and Aminah's eyes—one pair emerald green, the other dark brown and more beautiful than a doe's. He deftly avoided the appreciative glances from over-made-up eyes and leaned against the polished timber bar. He ordered a soft drink rather than an American beer. It was a taste he'd never acquired. He recognised the needle-in-a-hay-stack nature of the task ahead. Green, blue, brown, grey. A kaleidoscope of eye-colours taunted him.

Rashid's scowl discouraged the pack in the main, but there was one more brazen than the rest, her plumage more colourful and her age more befitting that of his mother.

"Well, hello to you handsome." She held a half-full glass of champagne high to avoid being knocked. "How is it that you're alone at the bar? Come upstairs and join us. Young women haven't got a clue these days."

"Not a clue as to what?" Rashid struggled to disguise his displeasure. He had no taste for overly confident, older, *married* women, he thought as he observed the shiny gold wedding band on her finger. And no taste for adultery. At least, *this* woman was upfront about her marital status.

Her smile told him she intuited his opinion and cared not a hoot. "I know a quality man when I see one."

"Perhaps they're more interested in quantity." He relaxed a smidge as he recognised camaraderie rather than a desire for conquest.

"Size matters, you think?"

"Where there's smoke there's fire."

"Why are you overheating down here? There's fresh air aplenty upstairs. Why don't you come up and join us?" She pushed on through the throng of people, looking back over her shoulder, her smile beckoning him to follow.

"Why not?" Maybe his prey had a penchant for the night air.

The entry to the next level was closed for a private function, but she waved to the security guard and led him up the carpeted stairs. How the woman navigated them in her over-high orange heels he didn't know. Practice, he'd guess. She was very at home in her surroundings. A blast of cool air met his brow and he breathed out in relief. The hub of voices was louder here, the music marginally less deafening. The night sky provided a canopy, lit in part from the city buildings that towered around them. Open-flame torches threw shifting light and the noise of the traffic throbbed below.

His guide was a colourful lure. With her white-blonde hair, she stood out in a crowd as much by her personality as her attire. In less than a moment, she'd had him sussed.

She flashed him a smile and beckoned him towards a high table surrounded by stools and people milling around on their feet.

"Look what I found downstairs," she boasted with a grin.

"I have a treat for you." Nola's words were a whisper in Jemma's ear.

Jemma turned from the person she'd been talking to and… nearly fell off her heels. Her body reacted like a fuse to flame. Her *treat* wore a grey suit and it fit him to perfection. Fine fabric over well-honed muscle. A white, white shirt; raven-black hair and tanned, olive-skin. His dark, sexy eyes captured hers with a focus that sapped the strength from her limbs and the moisture from her mouth. He looked—remotely—like Zahidah's sovereign prince. But Prince Rashid in a bar in New York? Ridiculous, she chastised herself. Not possible. Not probable. Not even sane. With a desperate swig of her drink she teetered on the edge of a stare more ruthless, more dangerous, more blade-sharp than a knife's edge.

Not five seconds ago, she'd forced herself to smile, to engage, to ask questions, but her heart wasn't in it. Now the bodice of her dress seemed too tight and the air too thin. He greeted her with polite aloofness and her voice went the way of the moisture in her throat. She grappled with the useless muscles, managed a wan smile and turned back to her conversation, except her words were gone and her thoughts spun. Her body recognised him. Every cell. Every fibre. It was him.

Somehow, Rashid was in New York. At the same bar. But he showed no sign of recognition. Her companion moved closer to make himself heard, his mouth a short distance from her ear, and she took a defensive step backwards, slamming into a wall of muscle, hard and heated. Tectonic plates shifted as big hands captured her waist and steadied her.

"Is everything alright?" The husky male voice whispered with conspiratorial closeness. The deep cadence of it resonated through her body and she found herself on a precipice of longing she fully blamed on the fizz of the champagne in her blood. His musky male scent promised all kinds of wicked. Get a grip. She had to leave. Now.

"Yes, thank you." Only once before had her body reacted like this to the mere touch of a man and her mind shifted to another bar, another night. A night of… amazing, earth-shifting sex. She didn't believe in love, but that night? She'd wanted to. It was a long time ago, she assured herself. Even if it was him, which was crazy, he wouldn't recognise her. She'd changed her appearance. Besides, the bar was dark. She felt light-headed. Wobbly on her heels. She needed water. She needed to sit down. She needed to go.

Before she'd done more than lower her glass to a table, dark spots overtook her vision and the floor seemed to tilt. She found herself cradled against steely muscle, red hot and branding, and the high-pitched thud in her ears shifted from a percussion to a roar.

"It's not every day a woman falls into my arms."

Her eyes fluttered open and his smile was there, right there, with those sinfully delicious lips she yearned, yearned to taste. His cheeks were flanked with the slightest of dimples in sexy man-shadow. Desire arced through her body. A body that felt as light as air. As warm as summer. He was carrying her?

She vaguely heard Nola's concerned voice in the background, his assurances he would find a place for her to lie down.

"I'm okay. Thank you. You can put me down now." Dark, dark eyes. Concern in their depths. If he didn't put her down, her heart would seize altogether, and he'd have to lay those incredible lips against hers to force air into her body. Lucky her legs didn't have to support her weight. Truly, Jemma? And then she remembered. He wasn't just a tall, dark and handsome cliché she'd met in a bar—her gaze raked the perfect proportions of his face so close her breath must fan the square line of his jaw, her very jerky, erratic breath—okay, it was him, it had to be him, which her brain, her addled brain, told her was ridiculous. Paranoid. Oxygen deprived. *Water.* Her throat was as parched as the desert. The Zahidan desert. And there it was again. The olive skin. The dark man-shadow. The black sinful eyes that blazed with desire. For her. Get it together, Jemma. In this man's arms? Why wouldn't he put her down?

"I'd take you outside for some air, but we're already outside, so I'm angling for a seat." People parted like the red sea before Moses, as if the mere presence of the man was sufficient to bend their will. Miraculously, he lowered her onto a couch, and she found herself horizontal. Oxygen rushed back to her head and her face flushed with burning heat. Or was that embarrassment? No man should have the power to do to a woman's body what his touch did to hers. For the second time, she thanked her lucky stars she didn't have to stand.

A glass of water appeared, and he held it for her to sip, his hand strong and broad, capable, and distracting. Hell. Even the sight of his hand sent a flurry of reaction through her body. She was pathetic. How long had it been since she'd had sex? No, she couldn't afford to think those kinds of thoughts when his gaze seemed to pierce right through to places dark and secret. Desire had her vision swimming and her breath catching. She'd never figured herself for the kind of woman who would swoon at the feet of a man. Twice. Surely that lesson had been learned.

"Are you going to tell me your name?" he asked, white, white teeth flashing against firm, plump lips, the slightest hint of an accent. "Since I caught you and saved you from cracking your beautiful head."

No. His words brought tears to her eyes. What was wrong with her? Since Aminah had disappeared, she'd lost the plot. *Drink the water, say thank you and get the hell out of here.* Which was good in theory, but impossible in practice since his mere proximity had her at risk of falling off her heels again. She lifted herself to sit and studied him over the rim of her glass. As suspicion, then certainty, fought with pheromones, she struggled to find her words.

His eyes narrowed marginally as if to assess her health and he placed his palm over her forehead. No doubt he was used to women falling at his feet, all pliable and willing. She was not so used to being the fall-ee. Nor was she the pliable type—usually—although a careful assessment of her body suggested there was not much resistance there. As for willing? Hell. *Drink the water, Jemma. Say good-bye. Thanks for catching me. Have a good life. And go.*

"You do remember your name, don't you?"

"I don't think I banged my head..." My *beautiful* head. His words sang in her ears and as their gazes snagged, she couldn't stop the skip in her pulse. Maybe she was a little lightheaded. "I need to go."

Dark as it was, she saw the rapid flare in his pupils, the escalation of his pulse at the base of his throat. His body, though casually relaxed, had the air of a rattlesnake about to strike, potential motion in every muscle. She forced lazy into her perusal of his outstanding masculine form. She had to leave. Now. He had danger written all over him. For heaven's sake, Jemma. If it was Rashid... it was Rashid. How had he found her? Get a grip and get the hell out of here. Now.

"I'm Raz," he murmured with a look that pierced right through to her bones.

Raz. The name was as exotic and sumptuous as pomegranate. Her sense of drama was in crazy mode. Why would the sovereign prince of Zahidah be trawling a bar in New York City? The very same bar at which she happened to be cooling her heels? Because he had come for *her*. But he didn't act like he'd found her. He didn't recognise her. *Yet.* Fear fought with attraction. Anger with desire. Hatred with hunger. Every over-sensitized, hormone-engorged cell in her body was a betrayal.

"Well, Raz. Thank you for the water and saving my head from hitting the floor." Her pulse accelerated as primitive magic swirled between them and his gaze, both blistering and cool, held hers—relentlessly. "I'll be fine now. Thank you. I was about to leave anyway."

"I'll take you." Regal arrogance and bow-at-my-feet oozed from every pore.

Jemma took a long gulp of water as if the liquid could soothe

the craziness that stormed her senses. Raz took the empty glass from her and his hand brushed hers, leaving a fiery trail of oh-please. Her senses scrambled. What part of dangerous did she not get? Oh, blue blazes. How could her body betray her like this?

Not going to happen, she chastised herself with a jagged breath as he took her hands in his and drew her from the couch. Oh, my. She ignored the mass pleading in her body as he assessed her stability, his careful attention draining the blood from her head. Her woozy head.

"Thanks, I'm fine. Truly." Or she would be if he would just let her go.

"You don't look fine. Let me get you a cab. Would you like me to see you home? You look pale."

He scooped her into his arms. Crap. That whipped her senses into a fury. His stubble-roughened cheek brushed against her forehead and his hot breath skated over her skin. Her cheek rested comfortably against smooth cotton and solid muscle, and her head filled with nonsense. With the steady beat of his heart against her ear, she felt stupidly safe. He smelled of warm vitality. Her blood heated. Flared. Caught alight and blazed. She should demand he put her down. She should...

"We'll just say good-bye to your friends and get your bag." His voice was a husky torment, a low growl against hypersensitive flesh. Who would have thought that words, plain old garden variety words, could be so evocative? Yet they played over her senses, warm and spicy on a shallow gust of breath, and settled around her like a comforter. Hell. This was chemistry. Pure chemistry. All the more dangerous for the care and compassion it came wrapped in. A chemistry that was volatile and unstable at room temperature, let alone under provocation. She needed to walk away. Leave well enough alone. Another breath shared. Another savoured. His eyes were full of secrets. Like he was privy to things the rest of the world wasn't. Promises. As if a kiss from him could realign the planets.

She balanced there, caught in the eye of the storm. Gone was the thrum of voices, the growl of traffic, the outer world. Silence without—a cacophony within with every craving lurch of intimate muscles.

"How much champagne have you had?"

He thought she was drunk? Her cheeks flushed with embarrassment.

"I can walk. Really. I haven't had much. One full glass. A sip of another. I can get myself home." But she hadn't eaten much, and her tummy chose that moment to growl a different kind of hunger.

His eyebrows quirked. Jeez. The muscles at her core tweaked and the fine hairs all over her skin lifted and resettled. "Maybe you need to eat? Do you feel up to it?"

"No." Too quick. He'd think her rude and she rushed to soften the rejection. "Thank you, but no. I appreciate the offer. I need to go home." Now, if he'd just put her down, she'd be able to think.

Nola met her eyes, her gaze deep, as if to assess her well-being.

"I need to go home. I'm not feeling great. It's late. You two enjoy Bora Bora. Travel safe." Nola smiled and raised her glass in farewell. Brad winked. Damn. The devil had her in his grip and her best friend had no clue.

Chapter Three

A taxi pulled up in front of the bar and Rashid captured the door handle. He opened the door and helped the woman into the back seat, studying her too-pale face. Her blue eyes, summer sky blue, studied him back and his body tightened under her gaze. So like another woman. Impossible. *That* woman was married and lived in Australia. He couldn't think of *that* woman without seizing his brain circuitry. So, they were alike. Yet not the same. That explained the fascination. Catherine's eyes were a colour he'd never forget. Turquoise like a sun-kissed tropical sea. Her hair as red as the setting sun. He had no place thinking about *Mrs. Catherine Somebody-Else's-Wife*. His heart lurched and the bitter taste of betrayal left a distaste for the Western way of life. Still, his body wanted… wanted.

Duty came first. It always had. He had other things on his mind. Like finding the woman who'd stolen his sister. He took a deep, bracing breath of night air and closed his mind to the temptations that swirled between them. Sex was off the agenda, no matter how appealing she felt in his arms. No matter how appealing she looked with her tousled siren-like hair and plump lips promising all kinds of magic. Answering desire was there in the pool of black that fast obliterated the sea of blue, but her chin had other ideas like back-off. A woman as smart as she was beautiful?

"Good-night, Raz. Thank you for seeing me to the cab. It was nice to be caught by you. Thank you."

Her tone was assertive, but her chin quivered as if emotions brewed just beneath the surface and he couldn't quite stifle the urge to brush his lips across hers in farewell. The world tilted on its axis, the contact moving from casual to sensual to seductive faster than it took the driver to clear his throat. Rashid ordered himself to release her, to strap her in nice and tight, and step away. He had more important things on his mind, like a woman with cat green eyes and a sister to find.

"You didn't tell me your name."

Her pupils, not moments before spread with desire, contracted and she folded her arms around her as if to shield herself from the cold. Except it wasn't cold. It was a balmy summer night in New York City, albeit cool by Zahidan standards.

"It was nice to meet you, Raz. Thank you again."

"Good night. It was nice to meet you, too." *It was nice to meet you.* His words mocked him as he closed the door between them and stepped back from the vehicle. He watched it edge into the snarling traffic and then realised she hadn't told him her name. Her attention was riveted to something in the distance and he waited, hoping she'd look back. The ring of the phone in his pocket pulled him from the fog of enchantment. He had a job to do.

"What is it?" he snapped, the tension in his body demanding an outlet. He had no desire to go back into that cramped, heaving mass of people.

"You found her!" Raz's vision shot back into focus. Had

Ahmed, his head of security, lost his wits?

"No, not yet."

"But the GPS on her phone suggests she was right there. With you. I'm on my way down." His voice was a yell against a cacophony of background noise.

"That's not possible." Rashid scanned the area in front of the bar. A man and a woman stood nearby in a close embrace, completely enamoured with each other. Could that be her? He couldn't see the colour of the woman's eyes. He slipped the phone back into his pocket and moved towards them.

"Excuse me. Would your name be Jemma?" The woman turned and his heart sank. Brown eyes, sultry and appreciative. "I apologise. I thought you were someone else."

"That's okay," she said with a smile, her attention returning to her companion.

Rashid prowled the pavement with frustration. So close. How could he have been so close and not seen her? Because he'd been distracted. Pathetic. His mind returned to his mystery woman. Her eyes were blue. Sultry, take-me-to-bed blue. Not firework green. None of it made any sense, least of all the rampant sexual need that charged through his veins. He was not in the habit of picking up women in a bar; hell, in Zahidah, he was too busy working and... his mind veered to the one and only time he'd picked up a woman in a bar and allowed himself to succumb to desire. That night had changed him. He'd wanted a future with Catherine, a future that belied his promised betrothal—briefly—until he'd woken the next morning and discovered her note. The knife edge in his gut sharpened.

He paced and strove to control the demons in his head until Ahmed joined him. The older man closed the distance between them, his breath short and rasping.

"She was here. Not a metre from you. I thought you had her." He struggled to catch his breath, his hands on his knees. "I went to the bathroom and missed you leaving."

"It doesn't make sense. The only woman near me was a woman I helped into a cab after she fainted."

"Well, she's moving away from us. She must be in a vehicle. Did anyone else get into a car? A taxi?"

"No, but her eyes were blue, Ahmed." Rashid stared at the red lights of the vehicles flashing by. How had he missed her? Had he been so blinded by attraction that he hadn't seen her get into a taxi? He didn't think so. What did it mean?

His mystery woman had been in a hurry to leave. Alone. She hadn't told him her name. Why? Because she was Jemma. Because she'd recognised him. He was a public person. She'd know what he looked like. How had she changed her eye colour? Coloured contact lenses? Hell, the woman was savvy.

"We'll hail a cab and follow her. I have her location. She'll lead us to her home, and we can apprehend her there." Ahmed was all business as he flagged down a passing cab and held the door open for Rashid.

"Her eyes were blue, Ahmed. I didn't make the connection." Rashid cursed himself as he climbed into the worn leather interior, his nose scrunching against the stale smell of cigarette smoke. He raked his hands through his hair and closed his eyes as he tipped his head back against the headrest. He hadn't slept for two days. Jemma had invigorated him—tricked him—and he'd momentarily forgotten his fatigue, but now exhaustion weighed upon him. "If she's the woman who coerced Aminah into harm's way, I'll wring her beautiful neck with my own hands," he growled. Was she laughing at his stupidity? The

31

blue of her eyes had been summer-sky clear. No guilt or guile. There had to be a mistake. She couldn't be the woman he sought. But then, women were masters of deception and there was no reason why she would be any different.

"She's not too far ahead of us," Ahmed said with a grimace.

Rashid fought the rogue thrill of excitement. They'd found her and soon he would find Aminah. Was she okay? Worry fought with fury.

"We've found Jemma and we'll find Aminah." Ahmed leaned forward to direct the driver.

"Yes," Rashid replied. "Failure is not an option." Failure was not a word in his vocabulary. He cut it from his thoughts and discarded it. Success would be his. Aminah would be found and the wedding would go ahead. It was a good union and despite the actions of Kamil's daughter… the thought of her coloured his vision red… the sins of the daughter could hardly be laid at the feet of her father. Mohammed was a good man. He would be a good husband for Aminah. Aminah would find happiness and contentment as his junior wife, and Rashid would be free of his obligation. The oil deal would go ahead, and his country's prosperity would be ensured. But he'd never be free of Catherine. She'd led him into adultery like a white camel to slaughter. He'd never finish feeling like a fool. Yet still, she haunted his thoughts, not so much in images but in tactile fragments. A soft sigh here. A silken thigh there. Hair like flame. The turquoise depths of her eyes so crystal clear a man could dive right in and lose himself gladly. She refused to leave his dreams, no matter how hard he fought to banish her.

The car swung to the right as the driver changed lanes. Horns beeped and lights flashed as they hurtled through the darkness towards the answers he needed to find.

Jemma rummaged in the bottom of her bag for her keys, her heels precariously perched near the edge of the top step outside the entrance to her apartment block. Seriously? What was wrong with her tonight? She lowered herself to sit on the step and rested the bag beside her. The light bulb over her head flickered on and off, and she struggled to see into its depths. Take everything out, Jemma. Wallet. Phone. Hand sanitiser. Tissues. Pens. Truly? Had she left them somewhere? Had she rushed out and left them on the counter in the apartment? She tried to remember, but she couldn't recall. It was a blur. Her bag was empty. No keys. She tipped it upside down over her lap. Damn. What now? She dumped her things back in, before lowering her head into her hands, her elbows unsteady on her knees. How could she get in at this late hour of the night? Who should she ring? Would they even answer? There was no caretaker on site. Had her keys fallen out of her bag? Had someone taken them? Should she wait until someone else came home who could let her in?

"My damsel in distress—*still*, it seems." The gravelly tone of his voice had her head snapping up so fast she got whiplash. Dark, dark eyes, the same suit, the same cocky smile. If it wasn't for the pitch of the steps, he'd tower over her. What was he doing here? How had he known her address? She struggled to her feet, well aware of the hitched-up height of her dress.

"You followed me?" Her body trembled like a leaf in a storm. She gripped the hem of her dress and yanked it down.

"You make it sound sinister," he replied with a scowl, his eyes less chocolate and more chipped black ice.

"Why then?" Her skin was awash with the chill of his gaze, every pore tense and tight. Her bag lay on the ground beside her. Her phone was inside it... she broke the connection and assessed the distance in the flash and flicker of light. Too far?

"You're her, aren't you? Jemma Mason."

"What if I am?" Her blood zipped through her veins like a crazy-excited puppy, all skittish and erratic, and her eyes swung to the man dressed in black who waited behind him like a menacing shadow. "Who's your friend?"

"That's two questions and you haven't answered mine yet." His tone was acerbic.

"Raz *is* short for Rashid, isn't it? *Prince* Rashid." The breath she'd held tight since she first laid eyes on him whooshed from her chest. "Should I curtsy, Your Highness, or scream?" Faced with the devil incarnate, she was incapable of movement. Dangerous? She was crazy-mad at herself. She should be inside and safe behind closed doors. He could have huffed and puffed as much as he liked, but no, she had to be waiting, exposed and vulnerable, on the front doorstep. Way to go, Jemma. Her mouth tingled with the memory of his goodnight kiss and she swiped at it with the back of her hand. Not going to happen. Ever. Again.

"You're her, aren't you? Jemma with the green eyes, only yours are blue." His voice snarled around her, but she couldn't run, not with his henchman just below and the door locked good and tight behind her. Focus, Jemma.

"…the woman who *stole my sister*." His words hissed across her skin and pierced her ears. Loud, edgy and sharp.

"How dare you! *You* are the one forcing Aminah—*Princess* Aminah—to marry against her will. You are despicable. If you don't leave, I'll call the police." Her words were raw from not enough sleep and too much emotion. Pain twisted in her chest like a blunt knife. The strobing light made the whole scene surreal like reality and nightmare had blurred and she couldn't find a grip.

"Aminah is missing and *you* have something to do with her disappearance." His lip curled and she couldn't fathom how she'd found him attractive. Twice.

"*You...*" Jemma began, her words etched with pain on Aminah's behalf, "...have no right to force her to marry this man. He's three times her age. It's wrong. It's obscene. It's unconscionable." Her vision blurred and she swiped at the moisture. Perspiration beaded on her upper lip. The night was uncomfortably warm, even now.

His eyes flayed hers with diamond-hard fury. "That's none of your business," he retorted with regal indignation. "I'm here because *you* plotted against the sovereignty of Zahidah. *Now, where is she?*"

"I wish I knew." Jemma collapsed back down onto the step beside her bag. This didn't make any sense. Why would he accuse her of taking Aminah if he'd done it himself? Fear flickered at the edge of her vision or was that the damned strobe light. "You *didn't* take her?"

"No. Why would I? *You,* on the other hand, must know where she is." Anger was there in his rigid spine and tension oozed from every taut muscle. His brow furrowed into sharp, disbelieving edges.

"No, I don't." She enunciated her words carefully. He may be important in Zahidah, but he was just a man like any other. Well, maybe not like any other. "I think we've established that already."

His eyebrow lifted and her inner body tweaked and twisted like a marionette. It had to stop. "Your expectations regarding this marriage are unjust." Focus on the main issue, Jemma.

"Unjust? You're telling me *my expectations* are unjust?" He

35

nearly expired from his visible indignation. "Who the hell are you? You have no right to judge me or my decisions. You know nothing about leading a country." He glared at her, his eyes as black as sin. "There's not a snowball's chance in hell you weren't involved in Aminah's disappearance. What did you tell her? Was it blackmail?"

"You have it all wrong." Jemma dug in her bag for her phone.

"Don't even think about it," he threatened.

"You can't bully *me* like you did Aminah. You may get away with that in Zahidah, but you won't get away with it here. America protects its people, even women." She narrowed her eyes into a glare of her own, her vision swimming. "Even visitors."

"Damn right I can and I'm not leaving until you tell me the truth. All of it." His gaze sharpened into chocolate shards and the furrows in his brow deepened. The flickering fluorescent light sent eerie shadows across his skin from darkness to ashen white.

"I've told you already. I had nothing to do with her disappearance and I'm as worried about her as you are." She clutched her phone, her finger on the 911 emergency speed dial.

"By Zahidan law, you are guilty until proven innocent." His words were a growl, prised from the tight set of his jaw. His hands clenched and tension throbbed from him in waves.

"Thank God we're not in Zahidah where women are owned by men and sold off to the highest bidder. In America, you're innocent until proven guilty."

He visibly flinched with every word. He was his father's son and Jemma knew well of the king's vicious temper. Maybe it was unwise to provoke him.

"In my country, women are protected and cherished and

treated with respect. But then in Zahidah, women behave in a way that is worthy of respect."

Unlike the woman he'd met in a Sydney bar. She rejected the guilt. They'd had a one- night fling. It wasn't like she was in the habit of having sex with random strangers. Sure, they'd connected in a way she'd never connected with a man before, but she was not under any illusions of happy-ever-after. Not in her world. So, she might have bruised his ego in the process and gotten burned herself, but Sami's creation had been earth-moving and life-changing, and she couldn't regret it.

"In Zahidah, women are repressed and controlled by men, and that's not worthy of respect," she replied in tired argument.

"What makes you such an expert on Zahidan women?"

"I was born in Zahidah and spent my early childhood there." Too much information, Jemma. Don't let him unsettle you.

"You're a Zahidan citizen?"

"If being born in a country makes you so, but I have dual citizenship and no desire to live there." Actually, she'd grown to love the city over the twelve months since she'd been there with Sami, and the custom of wearing a veil made her feel safe. Sami loved the busy markets, the pristine sea, the ice-cream. Guilt blasted her like a Zahidan sandstorm. Didn't a man have a right to know when he'd fathered a child, however nebulously? But this man was a prince and that changed everything. He'd either disown his daughter or take her entirely and Sami too would become a pawn in her father's political games. Sami was better off without him. Wasn't she?

"You understand Zahidan?"

"Of course." She relieved her feet of her heels with an exaggerated sigh. If she was going to have to run for her life, she needed a more even playing field.

"You speak Zahidan?"

"Some."

"You had *something* to do with Aminah's disappearance." He eyed her suspiciously, his fingers raking through his hair in frustration. "You're the only lead we have." He looked on the edge of crazy, his perfect hair standing up on end, his features strobing from shadow to light. Pain gilded his words and he looked every bit the aggrieved brother as he sank down onto the step beside her.

"I didn't," she whispered. "You're the one who backed her into an impossible corner. Not me."

"If not you, then who?"

"I don't know. I wish I did." She fought the inexplicable urge to comfort him. *Don't soften,* she chided herself. He may have given her the best night of her life five years ago, but he'd sold his sister to his ancient neighbour without a care to the fact that his sister was not a commodity to be traded. Her head understood, but her body? It craved his touch. Even now. Her gaze shifted to Rashid's ninja friend and escape seemed remote. She wasn't responsible for Aminah's disappearance, but she would have been if things had worked out the way they'd planned. The thought gave her pause. Aminah knew her brother better than she did. Had she known he would track them down? Had she known Jemma would be in danger? It was a thought that sucked the breath from her lungs. Could Aminah be safe? Was it a ruse for her brother's benefit? Her mind raced with the possibility.

"Yours is the only number in Aminah's phone. No doubt she would have loved your friendship. She has very few female friends. Very easy pickings for a woman like you." His body was rigid beside her and radiated heat like the sun off the desert sand.

"A woman *like me*?" she blasted. "Not fifteen minutes ago, you didn't seem too put off by a woman like me." He'd been kind and chivalrous to a stranger. The two images clashed, and she couldn't make sense of the disparity.

"My sister's freedom is at stake. Her life. So, forgive me if I seem a little… abrupt."

"My friend is missing and from where I'm sitting, it's *your* fault." They were at a stalemate. Her mind raced. If Rashid wasn't behind Aminah's disappearance, she could have been kidnapped by crazed assassins or religious zealots or… criminals, murderers, thieves. Or she could have followed through with her suicide threat. The thought left a clammy chill on her skin. "Aminah's *life* could be in danger," she said in a half-strangled whisper. "We have to find her."

"I will find her." His gaze held hers for a long moment. She teetered on the edge of it, her body remembering the magical connection they'd shared. No. She pulled herself back from the precipice. Men couldn't be trusted. This one in particular. So far, he hadn't realised who she was. Not with her hair dyed honey-blonde and her eyes coloured blue, but that didn't mean he wouldn't.

"Then this conversation is over." Jemma struggled to her feet. "You need to go. You need to find her." She pulled the strap of her handbag over her shoulder and tightened her grip on her shoes, ready to run. She eyed the distance between freedom and Rashid's dark friend, who stood a discreet distance away.

"I do and I shall, but until Aminah is found, you will stay with me."

His words were a quiet command and her blood turned to liquid nitrogen. "I can't." She bit her lip. She couldn't explain

39

about Sami. Not without risking her safety. "Besides, you have my number. You can call and keep me informed." She eyed the sparse traffic. Where was a cab when you needed one? Curses.

"Why was I looking for a woman with green eyes when yours are sky blue?"

"I wear coloured contacts," she said with a scowl. "I like to change the colour of my eyes." Not that she owed him an explanation.

"Eyes are the window to the soul. What does that say about yours?" His gaze was edged with about-to-pounce.

"Yours are as black as sin and I'm not holding that against you." Her bravado was skin deep. Her mind grappled for solutions.

"What are you so anxious to hide, Jemma Mason?" He studied her carefully.

"I have nothing to hide." Except her plot to save Aminah. Except her daughter! Fear prickled at the follicles of her skin, shimmying up and down her spine like a trapeze artist on steroids. Her knees locked to disguise the feeble hold she had on her equilibrium. Her world pitched and lurched. *And* a tell-all book about to be unleashed on the world. Locked or not, her legs buckled like molten steel and the ground was like quicksand, but she fought the sludge. No way would she fall into Rashid's arms twice in one night.

"Your body tells me differently." His gaze raked over her.

She refused to entertain the residual attraction. It was as unwelcome as his interference in her life. "What do you want to know?" she asked with a forced sigh. "You don't believe a word I say anyway, so I'm probably wasting my breath." Indignation was good and conversation gave her time. Time to step down onto the pavement and eye the road for a means of escape. The quiet, empty road…

"Why are you concerned about Aminah's marital arrangement? What possible reason could you have for getting involved?" He followed, close on her bare heels.

This was it. Probably the only chance she'd get to defend herself. The concrete was as hard and unrelenting as his Highness beside her and she gasped as a stone pressed into the soft flesh of her foot. Aminah had saved Sami's life and for that reason alone, she would do whatever it took to help her. "Your sister…" she stopped and considered him. He probably wouldn't believe her anyway. "Your father must be worried about Aminah's welfare."

"He is." The black of his eyes stormed with hidden undercurrents. "Why are you evading my question?"

"Aminah is my friend. Is that not enough of a reason to stand up for her when her brother won't?"

"What is your point?"

"Aminah says you are your father's favourite child. A status you accept without question. Why do you think your father treats Aminah differently from the way he treats you?"

"Aminah is female and the youngest. I am male and the oldest," he said with exaggerated patience and a shrug of his shoulders.

"Yet you tell me the women in your country are treated with respect? Not so much in the palace, perhaps?"

"In Zahidah, husbands provide for their women and children. A father decides if a man is worthy of his daughter. It is our way." He sank his hands into his pockets, his back rigid.

"So, your father's happiness with the arrangement is more important than *hers*," she said with a soft sigh, her eyes shifting to the road. It was quiet. Eerily so. As if the road had been cordoned off, which of course it had. Rashid was the Prince of Zahidah. He'd have more security than a visiting rock star.

Silence fell between them until Jemma could stand it no longer and her voice shattered the quiet. "Are we done here?"

"Not nearly."

"Then maybe we could continue this tomorrow. I'm tired. It's been a tough couple of days." Her body felt like it had gone several rounds on a torture rack. "I don't suppose your man there is any good at breaking and entering?" She peered around him to the older man who stood on guard, bristling with pent-up action.

"I'd like to understand how and why you befriended my sister." His voice gentled and he paused a long while.

Jemma pushed herself to tell him the truth. *I needed a bone marrow donor to save our daughter's life and I came to find you.* "I met Aminah through her charity work at the Zahidan hospital. Your sister was very kind to me. I wanted to help her in return." She held his gaze for the longest moment, her insides doing flips. "Besides, it's wrong for a woman to be forced to marry a man three times her age."

"You have a poor opinion of me, yet you don't know me any better than I know you. Although…" he halted, his words slowing, his gaze settling on her face as if he grappled with recognition. "You do remind me of someone." His brow furrowed and he shook his head as if to shake the thought away.

Jemma's heart kathumped. She didn't need his questions or his compassion. His kindness was far more dangerous than his animosity and if he were to recognise her, he'd wonder why she'd come to Zahidah when she was supposedly happily married to a man in Australia. When he'd told her his name that night, he hadn't prefaced it with Sovereign Prince. She'd been away from Zahidah for too many years to make the connection. As the Prince of Zahidah, he could hardly acknowledge his daughter and even if he did, he would never take a Western woman for his wife. No. He'd discard Jemma like an unwanted strumpet and Sami would be brought up without her mother. That was a plight she was only too familiar with and she couldn't bear for her daughter to suffer the way she had. Nor would she want her to suffer the way Aminah had. The life of a royal princess had little to recommend it.

"I have a car coming to pick us up since you seem to have locked yourself out of your apartment. Most convenient from my perspective."

"Hah." She couldn't stop the false smile. "I'm sure your friend there..." or was he a figment of her freaked-out imagination, "...could deal with a locked door."

Rashid's gaze shifted from hers as a low-slung, black vehicle turned into the street, but his ninja friend's gaze picked up where his master's left off and there was no hope of escape. Rashid's arm encircled her and drew her towards the waiting vehicle, his manners out of keeping with the slight force that propelled her forward.

"We would do better to work together than to fight each other," he soothed, his touch centred on the small of her back, both noxious and delicious.

"I have no intention of going anywhere with you." Her tongue seemed thick and heavy and her grip tightened on her shoes. Her muscles clenched ready for flight.

"You can hardly sit on your doorstep all night. It's not safe," he reasoned as he gently edged her towards the open car door. Going with him was akin to sliding from a hot pan into open flame. "I'll organise some food. I know you're hungry and you can rest on the way to Zahidah."

"Zahidah? I'm not leaving New York City with you. No way. There's not a chance." She pushed against him. "Besides, I have a flight back tomorrow."

"As of this moment, you have no choice. I'm sorry, but I need to find my sister and you're the only lead I have. For now, you'll be treated as a guest."

"I can't go with you. I have commitments." Her thoughts spun. She needed to get back to Sami... she could hardly tell him that. Her chest heaved.

"You can rearrange them on the plane." His words were confident as he nodded his thanks to the driver who had opened the rear door.

Jemma struggled to slow the kathump of her heart and made to duck under the corral of his arm.

"That would be less than wise," he growled. "If you care about Aminah as much as you say you do, we need to work together to find her."

He looked every bit the bereaved brother. She glowered with frustration at the dark appeal in his eyes, every instinct urging her to run. But he was right. Perhaps they would find Aminah if they worked together. Aminah could be in danger. She could do this. She had to. With forced dignity, she took the last three steps alone and lowered herself into the plush leather seat, the scent of new upholstery and obscene wealth choking her. "If you could just get your..." she eyed the black shirt, black tie and black suit of his security guy, "...*friend* to open my apartment door, you wouldn't need to trouble yourself on my account."

"No trouble," he said with a glib smile and lowered himself beside her.

44

Her nerves jangled as the door slammed closed. Along with most of her options. More Ninja men appeared from the darkness and several shadows pushed through the locked door. No doubt to retrieve her things.

"And no choice it seems." She smiled with saccharine sweetness. "I see now what Aminah had to contend with."

"Sometimes, a young woman does not know what's good for her." His face was dark with moving shadows as the vehicle slipped into the night. "Sometimes, a man does."

Chapter Four

Not likely, Jemma grumbled to herself. She sat in silence, but her mind raced. She was stuck in a situation more worrying by the moment. No doubt his men would find her apartment and go through her things. Would they search her laptop? She had deleted every reference to the book as it came in. They needed the element of surprise to guarantee Aminah's freedom. It was an important strategy in their well-thought-out plan. And what of her photos? Her screen saver? She didn't want Rashid to see Sami and realise how alike they looked.

"We'll eat on board," he assured her as if sensing her discomfort. If she weren't so hungry, she'd refute the need, but it appeared there were some needs she couldn't will away. Others, she reflected, she'd never entertain again.

Rashid spent his time on the phone, speaking in Zahidan, the language now more familiar to her ears than it had been twelve months ago. Then she'd had to translate every word into English and her comprehension had been slow. Now, she could readily pick up the gist of his conversation. It seemed there was nothing new to go on. Aminah had disappeared into the night without a trace and there was no ransom letter to give any clues.

She stared up at the night sky; vast, dark and invisible beyond the artificial streetlight and let the worry wash over her like a depressing wave. A sob curdled in the back of her throat and her breath was jagged and sharp. She owed Aminah so much. Without her, she would have lost Sami to the acute lymphoblastic leukaemia that had struck out of nowhere. She needed to get back to Zahidah and once they were there, she had to convince Rashid to let her go. She would have to tell him her daughter needed her. She had to risk it. For the moment at least, Rashid hadn't made the connection, but he was perplexed. The incongruence of seeing him in a New York bar had thrown her, too. Not to mention his worry for Aminah. He was distracted, his mind grappling with the puzzle of Aminah's whereabouts. But his body recognised hers and her body recognised his. The memory of his touch drew her like a magnet. She wanted him. Still. With a hunger that paid no heed to common sense. It had frightened her five years ago and it frightened her still.

Jemma's gaze veered back to the people—light-washed and slightly unstable—crowded around late-night coffee and food vans as if the dancing or the alcohol or the kissing had created an appetite for something fatty and sugary. She felt strangely disconnected from the ordinary as if the scene before her eyes was set and rehearsed. Her tummy lurched as visions of hotdogs danced in her head. She glanced at the red traffic light that stopped their movement and entertained the idea of opening the door and disappearing into the black shadows, but what was the point? Rashid would find her. And then it occurred to her. "How did you find me?"

"I didn't know I had." His voice was quiet in the darkness.

"You didn't?"

"No."

"Then how did you come to be at the same nightclub?"

"Your mobile phone has a positioning device and I knew your number. But it was very crowded, and I was seeking a woman with emerald green eyes. Yours are blue."

Her mobile phone? Of course. She fell into silence, a silence that sat clumsy and awkward between them. Rashid seemed to fill the entire space, his proximity as stifling as the afternoon heat and her gaze blurred as she recognised the futility of fighting him. His security forces would find her wherever she went. There was cold comfort in the knowledge. They would find Aminah, too. But what if Aminah didn't want to be found?

No, Rashid would hardly have helped Jemma into a taxi or planted his lips on hers if he'd known who she was. She swiped at her mouth as if she could remove the tingling memory of how readily she'd melted into his heat. She'd wanted him. Even after he'd closed the door and stepped away. Desire for Aminah's brother? The very thought was a betrayal after all that Aminah had done for her. She needed to breathe. Steady herself.

"Why didn't you listen to Aminah when she went to you and pleaded for your understanding and compassion?" Jemma asked, her voice quiet. The man she'd desired, the man she'd known had been chivalrous, caring and compassionate. What she'd learned of him from Aminah and what she'd intuited were at complete odds.

"There is more at stake than Aminah's feelings. Aminah is a member of the royal family. A royal marriage has important political and economic ramifications. For many generations, my family has made choices that benefit our country. Aminah has obligations and a duty to Zahidah. As do I."

Jemma bit her bottom lip as if the bruising pressure could stop the words that came without caution. "I find it hard to understand how those obligations could be more important than your sister's wellbeing. Aminah threatened to take her own life before she'd marry Sheikh Kamil." Jemma waited to see his reaction, which was disappointingly slight. A frown. A ticking muscle in his jaw. Did he not understand the danger? "I couldn't stand back and let Aminah die."

His glare turned a darker shade of black and shadows slashed the square line of his jaw. "Why would you believe her?"

"Why wouldn't I?" Jemma parried, realising in a bone-shaking moment how much she wanted Aminah to be a part of her life. To be a part of Sami's life. And how much she feared losing her. She was family.

"Because your friendship is what? Twelve months old? Slightly less? You haven't known her for very long. Why would you think her threat was real?"

"Why would you think it wasn't?" Grief glittered at the edge of her vision like a desert mirage. "People do take their own lives, you know." Like Jemma's father who had succeeded despite her best efforts to help him. "I don't want Aminah to be one of them."

"I don't want to be having this conversation and yet here I am, in New York, forced to find the woman responsible for planting selfish egotism into the mind of my younger sister, who until now has always been obedient and humble as a woman should."

"I don't think you understand how desperate Aminah feels. She believes death may be her only escape. Perhaps she's right." Jemma adjusted the seatbelt where it cut into her neck.

"So why didn't she tell me of her plans?" His words were

49

tinged with what? Disappointment? Injury?

"Because you wouldn't listen. Because she believed this marriage was more important to you than her well-being."

"There is more to compatibility than physical desire. Sometimes the young don't know what's best for them. They benefit from the experience and wisdom of those who are older."

Was he repeating a lecture received? A lesson learned? "You sound like an eighty-year-old man. The modern woman doesn't want to be forced into a marital arrangement devoid of love and desire." Her voice squeaked on the last, because truly, desire raced in her blood and try as she might, she couldn't push away the memories. Her body heated at just the thought of his bone-melting kisses. Really, Jemma? Five years ago, his compassion had turned to comfort, which had turned to connection, which had led to more.

With her father in a coma after his final suicide attempt, she'd been advised to pull his life support. She knew it was what he would want, but to lose her father had hurt on so many levels. She'd gone to the bar to sit with the idea and Rashid had kindly asked if she was okay. They'd spoken together for a long while before the emotional connection had led to a physical one. Pure escape. She'd woken earlier than him and, like the proverbial Cinderella, had run away, leaving not a glass slipper, but a note of thanks with a PS designed to free him of any obligation. Besides, the intensity of her feelings had frightened her.

She'd buried her father and believed herself alone in the world until she'd discovered the precious memento of her time with Rashid. Sami had been a welcome blessing. A child. Her child. Their child. In all of her imaginings, she could never have pictured herself beside him, as distant as a stranger.

"When a man pledges to protect and cherish his wife," Rashid continued, his tone regal and patient as if explaining something to a child, "it *is* a promise to love. Desire is fickle and foolish at best, and readily sated."

"Without attraction, how can there be love? Respect and trust need fertile soil." She couldn't keep the shake from her voice. "Aminah fully intended to follow through on her threat." Memories clawed at her throat.

His gaze meshed with hers before focusing dead ahead, his body rigid, his hand with its royal crested ruby ring pressing hard into the soft leather of the seat as the vehicle turned sharply. Blood red, it caught her attention as it shone in the streetlight.

They were almost to the airport.

"There is much riding on this union," he said despondently, "and I believe it's a good arrangement for her."

"Yes, she told me."

They fell into silence for several long minutes and Jemma struggled to maintain her anger. He seemed distressed and genuinely concerned for his sister. Perhaps he would allow her to go to Sami if she explained about Sami's illness and ongoing recovery.

"I have a daughter, Sami, who has been very unwell. She's getting better but I need to get back to her." She caught her lip with her teeth and strove for calm. If he realised who she was? It would be fine. Her postscript had told him she was married. He'd just think she'd had a child with her fictional husband.

He eyed her as he might a scorpion in the sand. "We'll pick her up on the way through to the palace," he replied, his tone businesslike.

"You don't understand," Jemma persisted. "She needs to be

in her own home, not somewhere unfamiliar. That's why I didn't bring her to New York. She needs her own bed. Her own space. It has been only six months since she was in and out of hospital. She needs *me*." Her voice broke on the last word. This was the man who five years ago had listened so intently, so compassionately and calmly. He'd helped her make peace with the hardest decision of her life.

"And yet you were in New York, cooling your heels at a bar," he challenged. "Every bit the doting mother."

"I was there to celebrate Nola's wedding. It's the first time I've been away from Sami." How dare he question her integrity. Tears threatened and bile rose in her throat as a myriad of emotions washed over her. Guilt. Despair. Love. They choked her and she pressed her hand to her heart, willing herself to hold it together. She'd nearly lost Sami. The relief, the months of worry, the emotions she'd buried so deep inside her to stay positive for Sami threatened to rise. Seeing Rashid again had thrown her. Sami would be fine. Aminah would be fine.

"You didn't think to speak with me about Aminah's threat? Her mental health?"

"No. Like Aminah, I saw you as the enemy." Ironically, she'd discovered Rashid had been betrothed at the time of their tryst. He'd enjoyed a frivolous night with her before returning to his poor fiancée. She couldn't trust him. She couldn't trust herself around him. He'd messed with her mind, conjuring all sorts of fantasies which were just that. Delusions. Dangerous desires.

When Sami had become ill, she'd had no choice but to go to Zahidah and seek his help, but she hadn't needed it. Not when Aminah had come to their rescue. And she couldn't tell him now. Not when there was every chance, he would arrogantly believe Sami was better off with nannies and bodyguards than her own mother. Jemma couldn't risk it.

"Perhaps Aminah feared there would be repercussions for you if your rescue attempt failed." Rashid's words dragged her thoughts back to the present. "Do you think she could have staged her own abduction?"

"Perhaps," Jemma agreed. She observed the brooding man beside her. His mind was with Aminah. "It's a possibility." A very real possibility she acknowledged as the vehicle pulled to a halt at a security point and Rashid's staff dealt with the diplomatic anomaly of Jemma's departure. "But she may be in danger. As much from herself as anyone else." Depression was something she knew intimately. Her father had struggled with it for as long as she could remember. Her eyes turned to the airport lights. They were on the tarmac, headed towards a small private jet. How could they not question Rashid's intention to take her from New York to Zahidah? No doubt, there was some diplomatic treaty which allowed him to do as he liked. And they probably had her passport by now. The line between truth and deceit was very fine. No wonder Aminah felt paralysed and desperate enough to consider taking her own life. It was the only sure means of escape.

Jemma's throat tightened and her hands grew clammy as the distance between the vehicle and the jet disappeared.

"I should have listened." Rashid's rueful voice broke the silence. "Aminah pleaded for my understanding, but I was blinded by my own perspective."

His quiet words were far from what Jemma had expected to hear.

"Is that the truth?" Her tone was incredulous. Or was it a ruse to unsettle her?

"I expect it from those around me and from myself," he said, his square jaw silhouetted against the light from outside the vehicle.

"And yet you had me tried and judged before you met me."

"You conspired with Aminah. You are at worst a liar and your morals are corrupt." He counted off her sins with cold derision.

"You weren't complaining about my morals an hour ago," she reminded him.

"An hour ago, I had no clue who you were. Now I know you planned to lead my sister into danger."

"Your sister was *in* danger. I planned to lead her *out* of it."

"Your failure was impressive."

"No more impressive than your own." Frustration sucked at her. She yearned to throw his sins in his face, but her hands were tied. She couldn't say what needed to be said. Aminah was missing. Aminah was her priority.

"In my country, those who have been wronged seek retribution." His smile was like that of a crocodile facing a wayward tourist.

"Aminah is the one who has been wronged and from where I'm sitting, you're the one responsible. Besides, you're abducting *me* against *my* will. I want that clear between us. I was given no choice. No more than Aminah. Sound familiar?"

"You plotted against the royal family of Zahidah," he said, the car drawing to a halt.

"So, execute me." Her body shook and she took a deep breath to steady herself.

"Forty days in the desert should suffice."

Jemma's heart nearly leapt from her ribcage. What archaic law gave this man the right to sentence her to anything? "I am an Australian citizen. I have rights a Zahidan citizen does not."

"You are Zahidan, which gives *me* rights." His tone suggested he had no more to say on the subject. He studied her with an intensity that lifted every hair follicle on her skin. "You're an Australian citizen?"

Damn. His body had worshipped hers and the sexual energy that even now arced between them like forked lightning over the desert suggested that even if he didn't remember their night together, his body did. His touch was an invisible brand on her skin, one she'd never be able to erase.

"Yes." She wasn't about to help him connect the dots and she needed to distract him before he connected them for himself. "What if I did know where Aminah was?" The lie raised the fine hairs all over her body. She had to keep her wits about her. She was no good to Sami dead, her bones baked by the Zahidan sun. She had to find Aminah. And then she wanted out of Zahidah and Sami as far away from her father as it was possible to get.

"If that were the case," he continued, his voice so guttural it resonated deep in her belly, "...now would be a good time to say so." He released his seatbelt, his back rigid. Jemma's bravado collapsed with a whoosh of air from her lungs.

"I wish I did."

"So, you have no idea of her whereabouts?"

"None." The thought was like wet concrete in her veins. Aminah was at risk of self-harm. Her life was in danger one way or another. "I *wish* I knew where she was."

Jemma's breath was a staccato. Her eyes pooled with unshed tears and her vision blurred. She wouldn't cry. The whole situation had become more awful by the moment. She needed Rashid to find Aminah, but if he were to discover his daughter?

"I will find her," he promised, his voice softening.

"I have no doubt you will, Your Highness."

"Be careful, Thameen."

"I am not your precious," she replied impetuously. His gaze captured hers with hypnotic intensity and her heart thumped against the wall of her chest. He was stunning and powerful beyond her wildest imagination, but behind all of that, she sensed a vulnerability that drew her like a magnet. She fought it as she'd fight him. "I'm not your anything."

"You are my guest," he declared. "For now. The plane is ready for us." He nodded towards his security team.

"Yes, Your Highness." She'd aimed for dutiful, but the snark was clear.

"It's foolish to provoke the Prince of Zahidah."

"I'm not afraid of you," she said with bravado. False bravado. She was terrified of him. If he were to take their daughter, it would eviscerate her and there was no chance she'd survive the agony of it.

"You should be."

Chapter Five

The devil makes for a bad bed partner, Jemma cursed as she drew the fabric of her veil closer around her face. Heat flamed from the inside out and the outside in. It was hot in Zahidah. It was always hot in Zahidah. It was as hot as hell beside Rashid.

He strode across the tarmac like a lion, his white robes billowing behind him. Powerful. Proud. Purposeful. The furnace-like air was rich with the scent of spices and outdoor cooking. The heat roused distant wafer-thin memories of pistachio and rose water ice cream. She'd worshipped it as a child, almost as much as she'd worshipped her father.

Voices called in Zahidan, which sounded foreign to her ears after being in New York.

The wind swept the fine sand off the scalding bitumen and blasted her legs. She was grateful for the long dress she'd changed into on the plane. Her Western clothing would have done nothing to protect her from the searing sand or the late afternoon sun. Besides, her nightclub attire would have had her arrested.

"You will stay at the palace," Rashid said with command in his tone.

Jemma's pulse leapt like a frightened gazelle, but she steeled herself and dug deep for strength. "I need to go home to my daughter, Your Highness."

"Jemma." Rashid turned to consider her.

"Yes, Your Highness?" Her gaze met his with guileless enquiry, but inside, her heart hammered against her rib cage and a thousand wings of panic took flight.

"Your daughter is welcome to accompany us. It's your choice. Shall we pick her up on the way?"

"No, thank you, Your Highness." Her gaze dropped from his to linger on the watery mirage that rose from the asphalt and tears blurred her vision. The hot wind gave her an excuse to brush them away. The heat of the tar seared through the soles of her slippers. "Can I have my phone so I can tell her I've been delayed?" Her voice rose to combat the grab of the wind. "She needs to know when I'll be home."

"You can use mine." His voice was edged with frustration, his movements jagged as he shaded his eyes from the sun. "And Jemma?"

"Yes, Your Highness?" she replied dutifully, the fabric of her bodice too tight in the heat, moisture beading on her forehead as the sun-ravaged her. Every restricted breath seared her throat and she battled the panicky beast in her breast.

"Please call me Rashid."

"Yes, Your Highness, I mean, Rashid."

"You'd tempt the patience of a saint." His tone was as unyielding as their surroundings. She wouldn't last five minutes in the open desert without shade and water. She'd be dead in a day, no need for the other thirty-nine. And if Rashid were to find out about the book? About his daughter? Her body quivered like lime-water jelly. The desert option would look peachy. With ice cream on top. The ground was unsteady beneath her feet and she struggled to find her balance. Every step tightened the figurative ties that bound her, and her hands felt clammy as she fought the wind to catch the fabric of her skirt.

"Yes, Your High…" She stopped, remembering his request.

A sound came from deep in his throat, more beast than man and she got the clear message she drove him crazy. Good.

"Perhaps you'd do best to stay quiet," he said through gritted teeth.

"Yes, Your Highness." Jemma heard him sigh. Rather than walk behind him as custom dictated, she remained at his side. An attendant waited by the door of a black limousine. The royal insignia was gilded onto the Duco. The man's white robes billowed like a sail and he bowed low as they approached. Jemma's confidence leeched away. Rashid was a prince. She knew it at a conscious level, but at a deeper level? He was a man who once upon a time had comforted her and cherished her and taken her body with selfless adoration.

Jemma welcomed the rush of cool air as she stepped into the luxurious interior. Rashid moved to the other side, speaking to the attendant in a rush of Zahidan before catching his robes and settling in beside her. Her senses stormed and his proximity caused her more discomfort than the blistering heat. She turned her attention to the window and strived to slow the erratic beat of her heart, to steady her breath, to sooth the tempest that raged in secret parts of her body. She needed space. She needed to see Sami.

Sami. Her precious girl… golden skin, thick black lashes, eyes the colour of a turquoise oasis. A distinctive colour like the shallows of the ocean over pure silica sand. The same colour as her own. Jemma closed her eyes to better savour the blissful memory of her daughter's arms and legs wrapped around her in a hug. Sami's cuddles were heaven on earth. She breathed in, savouring the remembered scent of Sami's soft, precious skin and silken hair. She yearned to see her, to hold her, to go home.

Her eyes pooled with tears of longing and through the blur she saw the date palms and the sandstone buildings of the old city. What was she to do? She couldn't trust Rashid. She couldn't trust herself. Not around him. Rashid's staff had confiscated her phone. It was the only way Margie could contact her. It was the only way Aminah could contact her.

The vehicle moved through the lofty gates of the age-old palace. There were security men stationed on each side. Here, escape would be impossible. Jemma sat rigid with the strain of controlling her emotions. She couldn't let him know how terrified she was. She wouldn't give him that power over her.

Rashid sat upright beside her, his brow creased with concentration, his gaze directed ahead. A muscle ticked in his jaw. He hadn't shaved that morning and his face was dark with rough stubble. In Western clothing, he was a feast for the senses, but in the traditional white robes of Zahidah? Her heart lurched. He was gorgeous, but no amount of gorgeous was enough to entice her back into his arms. Not that he wanted her there, which suited her just fine. What she had was a bad case of physical attraction. Even now. Even when her mind knew better. She'd hoped... her breath snagged. Hopes were foolish. She'd dreamed... wondered if they could be a family. Somehow. Someday.

She turned her head with exaggerated interest to her surroundings. Gardens as lush as the fabled Garden of Eden bordered each side of the long driveway. She couldn't stifle her gasp as the palace loomed closer. She'd seen it from the distance, but nothing could prepare her for the immense size of it close up.

Gold-gilded domes and tier upon tier of sandstone walls, small balconied terraces, and ornate ironwork. It spoke of power, domination, and durability. Jemma's heart pounded and the thud in her ears was loud enough to drown out the sound of the car engine. She wiped her hands on her clothing and a myriad of butterflies took flight in her stomach. She felt smaller and smaller as the building loomed larger and larger.

What on earth had possessed her?

How had she thought she could go head-to-head with the prince of Zahidah? The prince of darkness, more like. The Dark Lord—gatekeeper to the world's oil supply—one of the wealthiest men on the planet. What had she been thinking? Had she thought she could expose his family secrets and destroy his plans for Aminah's marriage with no repercussions? He would have found Aminah and he would have found Sami. Damn the voice in her head. He didn't even know Sami existed.

Because she hadn't told him.

She hadn't told him because he was a prince. Because he'd had responsibilities. Like a fiancée. And a wedding. And a country to run.

But the fiancée and the wedding hadn't worked out. So where did that leave them?

Nowhere. He still had a country to run and he was still powerful to her powerless.

Sami was *her* daughter. *Her* baby. Royal life was too demanding, too strict, too cruel for a small child. Even if Rashid acknowledged Sami as his own, even if Jemma was willing to raise Sami in Zahidah to allow Rashid access, every visit would be a circus. Her daughter wouldn't be able to walk the street or attend school without a royal stigma. Bodyguards. Paparazzi. Sami would feel different. She wouldn't fit in. She'd be isolated amongst her peers. Jemma knew how that felt only too well and it was not what she wanted for Sami. But the thought gave her pause. Rashid had grown up like that. He'd woken every day to the burden of responsibility and loneliness.

No, she didn't want to feel compassion. She didn't want to forgive him. She wanted to hold onto the bitter emotions that kept her bones steely and her determination even more so. To empathise was to realise they had more in common than she'd thought. No. Sami was better off without him. Jemma was better off without him.

Her gaze shifted to the man who sat beside her, dark and stony still. He cared about his sister. She had to admit that. And one night, long ago, he'd cherished her and made her feel like a princess. Special. Like she was the only woman who'd ever moved him in such a way, which was fanciful and stupid and very unlike her. Sentimentality? Fresh tears welled in her eyes and she fully blamed Rashid as she turned away. When he gave a woman his attention, he did so completely. After her father's death, life had been dark, like an emotional eclipse. Her pregnancy had been an unexpected light in the darkness. Sami had given her hope. Love. Family. She owed Rashid so much, but could she trust him? If she told him the truth, would he take Sami from her? He was a prince. She was... nobody special. But she was Sami's mum and Sami was her world.

Rashid's life was eons from hers. Obscene wealth surrounded her. Jemma was so far out of her depth it was impossible to catch her breath. She could do this. She had to. Somehow. *Breathe.* She just had to find a solution. *Breathe.*

And hope he didn't realise who she was. *Breathe.* She felt spacey and light-headed. Too much in-breath and not enough out-breath. Slow it down. Damn. Don't breathe. Don't think. Don't over-analyse it.

The vehicle stopped and a man in an ornate uniform opened the door, bowing his head as he waited for her to alight. Her gaze swung to Rashid, who gestured for her to go first. He waited until she stood on shaky legs before joining her himself.

Rashid's view of her was quite clear. Any physical attraction between them was a flash in a smoking pan, already extinguished and put behind him.

"Thank you." She spoke in Zahidan, but the words were lost in a dizzy sensation that left her reeling as Rashid pressed his hand to the small of her back and propelled her towards the long sweep of tessellated tile steps. Massive urns stood sentinel at uniform distances, each filled with a tall green palm.

"You will behave as a guest should behave," he murmured. "You will treat the staff with respect. You will do as you're told."

"Yes, Your Highness."

"Jemma. If you say Your Highness in that tone one more time, you *will* fry in the desert. Am I clear?" he asked, his words grated through clenched teeth.

"Yes, Your..." Jemma bit back what had become a pleasantly provocative habit. "I apologise."

"You are the most infuriating woman."

"Perhaps one of your staff could drop me at my apartment and save you the trouble of my company," she said brightly, the solution to her problems coming in a glittering rush.

"You will stay here until we find Aminah and you will behave as a guest should."

"Then I need to check on Sami." Her hope deflated. "Could I

borrow your phone please?"

"Yes." He pulled a shiny, late-model device from his pocket and punched a passcode into it. "Would you like one of my staff to watch over her and keep you informed?"

"I'd rather watch over her myself," she said as she took the lightweight, glossy device in her hand. "Thank you."

"If you wish to visit her, we could go together."

His hand was hot against her back and her objection came out in a rush. "No. No, that won't be necessary. No need to trouble yourself. I could go with one of your ninjas, I mean, security staff. I'd hate to impose on your precious time. You have a country to run," she reminded him as if he needed reminding, which she was sure he didn't, given his previous lecture regarding Aminah's responsibilities. No doubt he took his own equally seriously.

"Jemma, until we find Aminah, we stay together. Besides, I'd like to meet Sami."

No. The thought slammed into her as if she'd been crushed by the hooves of the massive horse statues that reared on either side of the huge, ornate wooden front doors. She bit the word back, her body tense and her mind ricocheted from one catastrophic thought to another. No. He couldn't meet Sami. He would know. She was so like him. Jemma's slippers tapped against the marble floor and echoed through the vast space around her. The extravagance took her breath away. Massive columns and arches, chandeliers like waterfalls, mosaic friezes, huge tapestries and paintings in gilded frames. Giant arched windows framed manicured gardens with rows of palms and a myriad of pools, splashing fountains and statues. Jaw-dropping, gobsmacking, obscene wealth.

Bewildered and overwhelmed, she allowed Rashid to lead

her into a sitting room. She collapsed into a gilded, velvet chair of obvious antiquity.

"How do you breathe in here?" This wasn't a home… it was more like a museum or an art gallery or one of those ancient palaces with roped-off areas that tourists couldn't touch.

"Call Sami and we'll take some light refreshment until my mother has been advised of our arrival. We'll take our tea with her."

Jemma's nerves tightened and her spine stiffened. She was to meet the queen? Aminah's mother? Sami's grandmother? Her breath was too short, and she was assailed by another wave of light-headedness. Breathe in. Slow it down. One… Kathump, kathump, kathump. Too fast. Too strong. Two… Breathe out. Slowly. How could she look Rashid's mother in the eye, knowing as she did, that the king was not Aminah's father? Three… Knowing as she did, that his mother's secret would be exposed. Not helping. Not helping at all. The knowledge ate at her like acid washed down with a healthy dose of fear.

"Are you going to call?" Rashid asked as he poured lime water into a chilled goblet and handed it to her, his gaze studying her carefully.

"Oh, yes, of course, Your…" She stifled the phrase as his sharp gaze lashed her. She nodded, momentarily lost for words. "It's just the heat…" The lie sat uncomfortably between them. How had Rashid coped as a child in this place? Expectations, duty, and formality oozed from every shiny surface. At four years of age, Sami was still busy and up to mischief. The age-old treasures around here would be at significant risk.

Jemma took a grateful sip of the cool water, the sensation a welcome one as she broke the connection with his concerned gaze and lowered hers to the marble floor. Even the tiles were gilded—encrusted with real gold?

"Would you mind putting the passcode back in?" Jemma asked, as she dragged her attention back to the phone and her precious daughter.

"You must be tired after the trip." Rashid took the phone from her hand, his fingers brushing hers with velvet heat.

Jemma nodded. For women, words were an accessory. Here, men ruled, and women obeyed. This was Zahidah and this man was its leader. Hard. Demanding. Compassionate. And the father of her child.

Jemma followed Rashid with quiet obedience, her thirst quenched, her worry eased after speaking with Sami, but her mind was bewildered. She had no sense of what awaited her, and a foolish, blind faith in the man beside her. She feigned confidence, her spine straight, her eyes forward, but her senses were scrambled. Damn it. Stop. She had to focus. She was to meet the queen and she needed her wits about her.

They followed a high-ceilinged passage, ancestral portraits guiding the way, open flame torches in stone recesses providing light. Rashid's stride was loose and long. His chin was strong and determined, yet she sensed his tension. Or maybe it was hers.

Rashid knocked on an ornate wooden door and pushed his way into the room beyond. He held it open and beckoned for Jemma to follow.

She stepped into a heavily curtained, beautifully appointed room. In its centre, on a huge carpet, were cushions around a low gilded table laden with tea paraphernalia and petite delicacies. Candles flared in receptacles and long shadows stretched across the room from the huge arched windows as the darkness of night descended beyond. Jemma's gaze was captured by a huge portrait that hung in a giant gilded frame on the wall.

Aminah's mother.

"Ah, Rashid, you're home." His mother appeared from an adjoining chamber. Her affection for her son was clearly apparent as she cupped his cheeks and examined him before kissing him and drawing him into her arms. She savoured the moment before turning her gaze to Jemma.

"We have a guest," she said with a welcoming smile.

"Yes, this is Jemma."

Jemma studied the woman in front of her. How could she not carry her guilt like a thorny crown? The woman's soft gaze spoke of secrets closely held, but she carried herself with dignity, her jewels flashing and sparkling in the light, her silken robes embossed with gold. Cold comfort for a woman who knew her daughter was not her husband's child.

"Hello, Jemma. I am Nada. Rashid tells me you're a friend of Aminah's."

Her voice was polished to the nth degree, yet she sounded genuine in her interest.

"Yes, Your Highness." Jemma curtsied, her movement clumsy, relieved to break the connection and lower her gaze. This woman had done nothing to help Aminah, but where animosity stirred, there was also sympathy. Nada too had been forced into an arranged marriage with an older man, into royal life with all its privileges and barbaric customs. She was as much a victim as she was a perpetrator.

Nada's toes were tanned and adorned with gems. Jemma straightened from her curtsy and her gaze shifted back to Nada's face. Rashid's mother was beautiful from her perfectly pampered, rose-tipped toes to her kohl-enhanced, dewy-dark eyes. Intelligence was there in her shrewd gaze and courage. She had risked everything for a night of passion in the arms of a man she desired. She had risked her life.

Rashid stood rigid and dark beside his mother, a scowl furrowing his brow. He'd said very little during the flight and she'd welcomed his silence. It was better than feigned interest in polite conversation. She needed his help to find Aminah. Period. The more she got to know his Royal Highness, the more certain she became. Sami was better off without him.

"Would you like coffee?" Nada asked in well-pronounced English. "Or tea?"

"It was a long flight mother. Jemma might wish to retire to her room."

Perhaps it was because Rashid had stepped in and opened the way for her to make her excuses that Jemma felt the need to refute them. In reality, she had no desire to linger and every desire to retreat from the overwhelming wealth and the disturbing loss of equilibrium she'd experienced since Rashid had whisked her away in the dark-windowed limousine. Or if she was honest, from the moment his dark gaze had captured hers at the Red Hummingbird.

"I'd like a cup of tea, please."

Jemma settled herself on a velvet cushion and took in the oversized room. Her gaze snagged on the massive painting that dwarfed the rest. The light from the open flame torches quivered and danced across the oiled surface. The woman in the picture was a younger version of the woman who sat opposite her. This was a painting like none she'd seen before. Every brush stroke was enthralled. Every exquisite detail painstakingly captured. The depths of Nada's eyes nearly wept from the canvas, lush and exotic, liquid with desire and invitation. The fabric of her dress fell from one bare shoulder and her head turned towards the viewer with a provocative smile.

Jemma's gaze dropped to the intricately woven floor coverings. She grappled with emotions, raw from too little sleep.

Rashid lowered himself to a cushion beside her, his legs stretched out beneath the flat expanse of the ancient wooden table.

Nada poured the brew from a long-necked golden pot into small, gilded cups.

"Aminah was happier I think after she met you, Jemma. I thank you for being there for her. Did she speak with you on the day she disappeared?" There was a catch in her voice, but she busied herself reaching for another cup.

"No. I was in New York. Aminah didn't answer her phone when I rang, and I was waiting for her to return my call."

"Rashid said you and Aminah communicated often," she added, at home with the pleasantries and the social theatre.

"Yes, Your Highness," Jemma replied, desperate for a fraction of the woman's veneer.

"You live in Zahidah?"

"For the past year, but I move around with my work. My father was the same. We never stayed in one place for very long. I was born here though, and we lived here when I was a child."

"You speak Zahidan?" she asked in surprise.

"My Zahidan has improved since I've been here. I understand it well, but I'm not very fluent. English is my preferred language."

"How old were you when you left?"

"Five," she replied, the old hurt scoring her throat.

"Then you have memories of our country?"

"Yes, although not all of them are good. My mother and brother died here when I was very young, and my father struggled with his grief." She spoke of her past as if it mattered less than it did.

"Then you have roots in Zahidah that go very deep." There was compassion in the crease of her brow.

"Yes." Jemma took a sip of the fragrant frangipani tea. It was refreshing and sweet, and she enjoyed the pungent kick of it as it slipped down her throat. Her eyes closed to savour it. She was tired. More tired than she'd realised.

"Did Aminah have any reason to think she was in danger?" The queen's voice penetrated the throb in her head.

"None that she spoke of." Nothing beyond the danger of her approaching nuptials.

"Mother, we don't know who was involved in Aminah's disappearance or why. Jemma has agreed to stay here until we do. Aminah may try to contact her."

His tone suggested Jemma had a choice regarding her current predicament, which made her choke on her tea. When she regained her breath and released the hand she'd held to her chest, she refused to acknowledge him. "We usually speak every day," Jemma said quietly to Nada, "but I haven't heard from Aminah since the day she disappeared." Fear wormed its way into her thoughts. The unanswerable questions were relentless, and she swallowed them down with a gulp of tea. The burn was a welcome distraction.

Nada reached out and laid a hand on hers in comfort.

"Thank you for worrying about my daughter." Nada's gratitude was genuine. Did she think Aminah wasn't worthy of her friendship?

"Aminah is like a sister to me."

Jemma shifted her attention back to the painting. Nada's husband had no doubt been there, behind the painter. He would not have left his beautiful young bride alone in the presence of another man. Nada's heated gaze was no doubt for the man she'd married and not for the man who'd skilfully painted her image. No. The idea was crazy.

"If you've finished your drink, Jemma, I'll show you to your room," Rashid interjected, his tone soft, but authoritative. "We'll continue this conversation tomorrow." Since they'd arrived in Zahidah, his manner had become more superior.

"Yes, I've kept you from your rest. You must be tired." Nada pressed Jemma's hand and released it. "I apologise. I was anxious to speak with you."

"It was lovely to meet you." Jemma's smile short-circuited as Rashid reached for her hand, his touch sending a rogue wave of reaction through her senses leaving her discombobulated like she'd been picked up in the hazardous surf and slammed into the ocean-floor.

"Jemma?" Rashid's tone was impatient.

She rose on shaky feet. "Your painting is very beautiful."

"Yes." Her tone was wistful. "It was commissioned a long time ago."

With a bow of her head, Jemma retreated, anxious to avoid the heat of Rashid's palm against the small of her back. As the door closed behind them, she sighed with exasperation.

"Please don't touch me, it's…" She struggled to find the word she needed. Distracting. Provoking. "Annoying."

"I'll do my best." His tone was laced with humour.

"Thank you." Jemma glared at him and clenched her fists with frustration.

He considered her for a long moment before turning on his heels. She had no choice but to follow him down the lengthy passageway, her furious gaze on his broad, muscular back. No man had a right to wear a robe the way he did.

He stopped outside an intricately carved wooden door.

"This is your room. There will be a guard outside your door at all times. You are not free to leave without my permission or my company."

"Thank you, Your Highness." She bowed her head, a provocative slight in her tone, although her thoughts were with Aminah. "There must be an explanation for Aminah's disappearance. Maybe the bridegroom wanted out? Maybe he wasn't happy with his marital obligation?"

"I don't like where you're heading with this. You need to be careful what you say," he growled. "You're no good to her dead."

"There'd be no risk of that if you'd get on with finding her." Jemma stormed through the door and spun back to face him, every impulse demanding she shove the door closed in his face. Instead, she waited, her muscles trembling with the effort, her gaze captured by his. Emotions warred in the dark depths of his eyes. Pain. Grief. The anger dissipated. She found herself softening and her heart warming. "I know this is difficult for you, too," she whispered.

Rashid raked his hands through his hair, his tension obvious in the jagged movement. She had to crush the impulse to comfort him.

"I'm sorry, Jemma. It's a very difficult time."

He turned and closed the door behind him with a thud. She heard a key turn in the lock and groaned with frustration. How was she to help Aminah when she was locked away?

Her attention turned to the room around her. So much space. The ceilings were ornate and soared high above her. Her feet sank into a plush carpet that stretched over the polished marble flooring. A four-poster bed sat glamorous and luxurious on a large platform. The wood was polished and buffed, the bed framed by curtains of the finest transparent fabric pulled back with silken ties. She threw herself onto the pile of silk pillows and cushions and closed her eyes against the muted lamplight. Oh, what a mess. How had it all gone so frightfully wrong? They'd planned so carefully.

Fighting the heaviness that dragged at her limbs, she forced her eyes open and searched the room for her bag. There. Near an arched doorway that led into an ensuite and a walk-in robe. No doubt as over-the-top opulent as the rest of the room.

She foraged through her bag, but her laptop was gone. No doubt confiscated like her phone. She had no way to contact Sami. She closed her eyes and prayed for patience. Sami was okay. Margie would take good care of her. She opened her eyes and let her gaze trip from one beautiful treasure to another. Aminah was a princess. She hadn't fully appreciated that before. How could she have been so foolish as to think she could save Aminah from this gilded cage? There was no escape.

Chapter Six

J emma woke long after the sun's heat had reached its blistering zenith. The bed was like sleeping on a cloud, the room cool and dark. The nightmare of Aminah's disappearance was slow to penetrate the blissful fog of a night filled with vivid dreams. Dreams of dark skin across pale, a touch like magic, a desire that consumed her. Kisses that took her from human to Goddess. From Goddess to formless. Magic. Masterful. Mind-blowing.

The taste of passion lingered on her lips. Mmmmmm. And then it struck her.

Aminah.

She was in Zahidah.

What time was it? Afternoon? It couldn't be. She swung her legs over the side of the bed and made a beeline for the bathroom. The tub looked inviting, but she couldn't afford to linger. Instead, she twisted the tap in the shower and stepped under the cool spray. How could Rashid have let her sleep so long?

She didn't bother with Western-style clothing, instead opting for the more traditional dress of Zahidah. She wore emerald green contacts to match the exotic fabric of her dress. She couldn't afford to slip up. If he saw the true colour of her eyes, he would recognise her. If it weren't for his worry about Aminah, he might have done so already. Her breath hitched and the strength leeched from her legs. She sat down abruptly on a plush, upholstered chair. Aminah would be okay. She would be found, and she would be fine. Jemma would take Sami back to Australia and they would be safe.

Jemma looked around her. Aminah had grown up in this sumptuous, indulgent, crazy-beautiful palace, but the cost was too high. She rose to her feet, savouring the cool of the marble floor as she walked barefoot back into her bedchamber. She spied a tray of breakfast things on a round table. So, someone knew she was awake. Fruit. Danish. Tea. More English than traditional. More to her liking in many ways. She opened the heavy curtains and was momentarily taken aback by the heat and the harsh light that stabbed her eyes. Ouch. It was bright outside. It took a moment for them to adjust. As she sipped her tea and munched on some fresh fruit, she observed her surroundings. Through the arched French doors was an enclosed courtyard and a lush lawn dotted with orange trees. If she strained her ears, she could hear the splash from a fountain built into one of the walls. But freedom was nowhere to be seen.

Never had a woman gotten under his skin in such a way, leaving him fretful, furious and inflamed from the inside out. While she'd slept like the proverbial sleeping beauty well into the day, he'd tossed all night, his mind filled with her taste, her scent—his hands lost in the paradise of her hair—her slender thigh tossed across his. Pale skin on dark. He'd been hard with wanting her. Craving her. The woman was a temptress of the highest order. In the early hours of the morning, he'd given up and headed to his study. Work had helped to distract him, but he still harboured a raging erection. The last thing he needed right now.

The woman was an irritation.

In a foul mood, growing darker by the minute, he gave a cursory knock on Jemma's door and waited for her to reply before striding into her chambers.

She turned from her position at the window, her forehead creased with worry.

"Is there any news about Aminah."

He shook his head. "No."

"What if she gave up on me and…?" Her shoulders collapsed forwards and her body shook with emotion, her hands wringing together.

"There is no greater dishonour." The tension in his body ramped up another notch. "Aminah is not a fool."

Jemma's face was wet with tears, her gaze imploring. He couldn't steel himself against her. She got under his skin whether he liked it or not. He didn't like it and his compassion was a double traitor, given his mood when he'd stepped over the threshold.

"Come," he soothed. "Sit here." He took her hands and guided her to the table, lowering himself into the seat across from her, smoothing his thumb over the silken surface of her skin and cursing himself as his body reacted. Their relationship had gotten off to a fiery start and although his head knew things had changed, his body refused to listen. "Let's go over what we know. Aminah eluded my security staff and was out in the city at night for reasons unknown. She was pushed into a vehicle by persons unknown. Witnesses have confirmed this. She dropped her bag on the road, which enabled us to confirm her identification. There's been no ransom demand. Nothing to indicate this is a kidnapping. Until we have more information, we don't know who's behind it. Or she may have staged it herself."

"Did you go through her things?"

"Of course."

"Did you find her passports? A Zahidan one and…" she paused, "an additional passport?"

Jemma had plotted Aminah's escape with clever attention to detail. "No."

Jemma nodded, but went on in earnest. "She would have hidden them. How well did you search her room?"

"Well enough." His thoughts were grim. If Aminah had access to travel documents under an assumed name, no one would suspect anything if she boarded a plane. She could be anywhere in the world. How were they to find her if she didn't want to be found? Jemma was the key. His sister wouldn't leave her worried and distraught about her absence for long. Would she? Aminah was a twenty-year-old woman, but she was as self-absorbed as a teenager. Perhaps she hadn't thought about the repercussions for Jemma. Or perhaps she had. She was savvy and creative, too, it seemed. Perhaps keeping Jemma in the dark was the best way to protect her. "What name would she be travelling under?"

Jemma bit her lip and her eyes lowered before lifting to his. "I can't tell you. If she'd come to New York, she would have called me. I rang and rang her the day she disappeared, but she didn't answer or return any of my calls."

"So, you refuse to give me the information which might help me to locate her?" He almost choked on the words and his insides tangled with frustration.

"If she used the passport, it would be of her own volition, but I don't believe she would put me—us—through this without letting us know she was okay."

"You believe Aminah..." Her look had him softening his tone. "...would have called you if she could?" His body had no right to react the way it did to the feel of her hand in his. *Unhand her*—but his body wouldn't listen. His senses were feasting, gorging themselves silly on the feel of her soft, satiny skin.

"I'm sure of it."

"Why? Why do you believe she wouldn't take advantage of you? If she wanted freedom so much and you orchestrated her escape, why wouldn't she see the open door and make a run for it? Why would she wait for you to return from New York?"

Jemma's expression was pensive. Her eyes were back to witch-green today. More stunning than the photo he'd carried at the Red Hummingbird. She looked good in Zahidan robes. Her small hands fit into his like the missing piece in a puzzle and soothed like warm honey. Her skin was pale against the deep tan of his, more English rose than desert flora. She appeared oblivious to the fact that her hands remained in his. Her mind was on the problem of finding Aminah. She was used to looking after herself. He could see that. She intrigued him. As did her strength. Their interactions had been on her terms. Even now, she was dictating and directing from the top of her ant hill. She was different from any woman he'd known. Most were only too happy to have a man look after them. Or a man come to their rescue. He refused to think of Fadila and her lover.

"No, she wouldn't do that. We had a plan. Together." Her face was fierce, and she pulled her hands away abruptly as if she'd suddenly become aware of his touch. Her loyalty to

Aminah was admirable if that's what it was. His mind snaked to the possibility that it was all an act for his benefit. A way to weasel her way into his affections. To gain the upper hand until she could…what? Blackmail him into marriage? Seduce him? What was her agenda?

"I have my top men working on this. We'll find Aminah." His mind turned to the next problem. He would loathe leaving this woman in the palace alone. "Tensions between the hill tribes have ramped up. I need to go there to negotiate peace talks. It can't wait. I will be away for four days." He watched her pupils flare. So, she saw his absence as an opportunity. For escape?

"Pack your bags." What was he thinking? The last thing he needed was Miss Trouble Personified along for the ride. He needed to deal with the problem and get back. Without complications. There was enough tension in the mountains of Zahidah already.

"What happened to leniency?" Her chin lifted and her gaze held his with defiance.

"I'm not planning to abandon you when we get there." What kind of man did she think he was? "Although if you misbehave…"

"Fine." She stormed into the ensuite bathroom and he could hear her throwing things into her bag.

"Don't bother with a hairdryer. There's no power."

She stuck her head out of the vast room. "Don't worry. I'm used to roughing it. Being a commoner and all." She flashed him a facetious smile.

She was gone before he could make a retort. She was irritating—from the top of her golden hair to the bottom of her perfect feet.

"Pack robes rather than Western clothes," he called. "It's

hotter inland." Besides, he liked the look of her in Zahidan clothing. Very much. Perhaps he should demand she shroud herself in a tent. For both their sakes. "And don't bother packing the coloured contacts!"

"Yes, Your Highness; No, Your Highness." Her voice carried easily from the adjoining room.

Facetious. Mocking. Vexatious. If she called him *Your Highness* one more time in that lofty, aggravating manner, he'd wipe the smirk from her face with his lips. He wasn't likely to forget the heat that burned between them. Flames more like.

"Ready."

She was back beside him, her bag in hand and her camera slung over her shoulder. Her glorious golden-blonde hair hung loose and unruly. She dragged her fingers through it as if the action could contain it for longer than a nanosecond. He eyed the sunny strands and breathed in the tantalising scent of her. Something sweet and vanilla based. Gardenia? Honeysuckle? He couldn't place it. Nor could he forget it. It was distinctly Jemma and it stirred him to no end.

She looked confused. "I thought we were in a hurry."

"We are. We'd better say farewell to Nada and get on the road. I want to get a good way before we set up camp."

"We're driving?"

"No, we're going by camel train."

"You're not serious," she reacted. "Don't you have a helicopter at the ready, being the richest man on the planet and all?"

"Not this trip. I need time to think and I find the open desert inspiring." He saw the understanding in her eyes. "We'll four-wheel drive it."

"With air conditioning, I hope."

"It's got windows that open."

"A rotisserie?" she jested, her intelligent, jade-green gaze roasting him with a single glance.

"I do like my women…" He stopped to give it some thought. "Heated," he finished, his voice cracking on the last. Wicked wanton woman. She'd left him thinking things he'd rather not. Sweat rolled down the centre of his spine. Damn her. He refused to allow her to unsettle him. Or distract him. There was too much at stake and he didn't trust her, although she deserved an Oscar for her performance as the confused and distraught friend, but it would take more than a great performance to convince him. If it was marriage she was after, she'd be very disappointed.

"I do like my men—inflamed," she replied and gave him a provocative look over her shoulder as she swept from the room.

He wouldn't go there, not if she was served to him on a platter. So, she knew what she did to him and found it amusing. He'd give her amusing. Had any man ever said no to her sexual lording? Probably not. Well, she'd met her match. Bring on the battle. He was more than capable of controlling his animal urges.

When he wanted to. And the jury was still out on that particular point.

Chapter Seven

Rashid had clearly had fun at her expense. There was air conditioning in the vehicle, but the man threw off enough heat to bend metal.

"I'd forgotten how the desert goes on forever." Rashid's henchmen had packed her camera and her gaze shifted from the photo on the small screen to the terrain beyond her window. Windswept, inhospitable and deadly. "Do you truly leave people out here to die?"

"Maybe a century or so ago."

"Forty days in the desert?"

"Your sins deserve no less." His brow lifted.

The quirk sent a provocative wave through her nerve endings, especially those secret womanly ones that refused to listen to reason. Rashid may be dark and sexy in a piratical kind of way, but he was judge and jury in her life right now and she'd do well to remember it. As soon as Aminah was found, Jemma planned to be gone. It was only a matter of time until the book was ready for publication. Aminah needed the book to negotiate her freedom, but if those negotiations didn't happen soon? It would be too late to stop the book from hitting the shelves. They were playing with fire. A very dangerous fire with very real repercussions for the royal family.

"My only sin is caring for a friend," she answered, her insides doing flips as the intensity of his gaze sparked something crazy inside her. It was a crazy she recognised. One that had led her to throw caution to the wind and get up close and personal with a man she'd just met. It cut straight through the rest. The disappointment. The fear. The longing. It communicated with something raw and elemental inside her.

Damn. She fidgeted on her seat. Really? Even now? What didn't she get? She needed to set boundaries. Draw a line in the sand—a moat more like. With marksmen and battlements. No way could she act on this simmering attraction. No. Not going to happen. Besides, he didn't remember her. The fact that he didn't recognise her should have doused any remaining fantasies about their night together five years ago. It had been meaningless, mind-blowing sex and nothing more. Except it *had* led to more. It had led to Sami and Sami was her world and for Sami, she owed him everything.

"Perhaps we need to discuss this…" Damn. Did she really need to bring it up? Too late now. She'd left the half-started, awkward sentence unfinished and now he was looking at her expectantly. Damn. She needed to name it and shame it. Get it out into the fraught space between them. It was there anyway. Flushing her skin with heat. Leaving her heartbeat, erratic and furious. His gaze burned with the same need.

"…Heat between us." Heat? It ravaged her body like wildfire leaving her fretful and breathy and hell, some traitor inside her still yearned for his touch. "And… *put it on ice*." The last part required an inordinate amount of effort as if she were dying and the words had to be said before she passed.

His gaze lingered on her face, before sliding to her body and rising back to capture the wayward wishes that must have danced there.

"Jemma, we're in the desert. There's no chance of ice out here…"

The concentration in his gaze was so intense it left her mouth dry. She sought to moisten her lips with her tongue, but his gaze followed, evaporating the cool relief before she had time to savour it.

"…Perhaps a more controlled approach is needed."

There was nothing controlled about his gaze and what it ignited within her. Her cheeks flamed. Damn. It had to stop. It was all fanciful thinking and treacherous at that. Way to go, Jemma. Give him a bit more encouragement. "No flames on this side of the vehicle," she lied, wishing for minions and a fan.

"Do you want to put that to the test?"

"No, thank you." Retreat. She knew when to hunker down and take cover. His brow furrowed and his facial expression thundered and growled like a desert storm. The air was decidedly stifling, and Jemma lifted the fabric of her robe to fan her skin. Her gaze veered to the window and the passing sand hills, her thoughts a jumble of unhelpful platitudes.

The vehicle lurched in the run-away sand, the motor revving, and her heart leapt. It was alright. There was no danger—*out there*—none at all. But in here?

"Perhaps the best way forward," he continued in a voice as smooth as Zahidan silk, "is to indulge it. It will no doubt burn out fast and furious once appeased, and then we can put it to rest. What do you think?"

Jemma's breath jammed in her throat. She tried to assemble the words she needed to remind him of the past. To remind *her* of the past. Hell, look where that had gotten her. Appease?

Burn out? Not in her experience.

"I think we have enough problems already," she managed through lips swollen with the mere idea of passion, her gaze lingering on the firm flesh of his mouth before hurrying higher to meet the intensity in his eyes... eyes filled with sexual sorcery and a hint of humour. Salacious hunger. For her.

"Is that a 'for' or 'against'?"

Sensation gripped her intimately, rippling out in concentric circles until her whole body was at war with her thoughts. There was an answering flare in his pupils, and she swallowed against the arid conditions in her throat. Every muscle tensed in preparation for flight or fight. Her gaze swung from his to the relentless dunes beyond the window.

Flight was out of the question.

"*Against,* Your Highness. One taste was enough. Too rich for my palate." Cocky back-at-you was her way of dealing with awkward.

"Oh, but you haven't *tasted* yet..."

Oh, yes, she had, and she salivated—shamelessly—at just the memory of his rampant assault on her senses. Fight, she demanded herself. Now. "What about Aminah?"

"So far, we have no leads, but my best men are working to find her." His gaze was searing, like the hot sun on her skin. "In the meanwhile, a gracious host would tend to your needs. You are my guest after all."

There was hungry invitation in every syllable.

"Your prisoner, more like." She tried to grumble, to admonish him, but her mind was on the desire that twisted inside her like a level five tornado. Her body communicated with his—shamelessly—and whilst her words and manner were loud with resistance, her body was liquid with musky invitation. And did she mention that level five twister? It rampaged through her senses, leaving her body swirling and spinning and simmering with just what swirled and spun and simmered in those gorgeous eyes of his. Damn. Don't do it. Don't soften.

"Semantics, Jemma."

Her name was a purr on his lips. A velvety-soft seduction. His eyes were like magnets and she found herself unable to shift her gaze, unable to stop herself from falling into their dark depths, her body tilting towards him as he moved towards her. Her mouth craved his possession, the warmth of him like an aphrodisiac. Stop. Now. Before she couldn't.

"Not wise, Your Highness." The paradise of his lips was a nanometre from hers. His breath was hot and heavenly and promised all kinds of great. She pushed back against the force of him, broke the intimate connection and pulled away. She found her hands imprisoned in his. His heat invaded her like a battlefront, sending arrows of sensation to her very core. She wanted him so much it hurt.

"Your body betrays you." His words were a soft temptation against her lips.

"Semantics, Your Highness."

"You have a smart mouth, you know that?" He pulled back enough to gaze into her eyes.

"Oh, you have no idea how clever it is," she parried, her gaze locked with his. Where had that come from? Seriously? She could see she'd hit her mark. Too easy. His pupils flared, he gulped for air, his hands tightened on hers. The muscles in his forearms clenched under his deeply tanned skin. She shifted her gaze to the desert behind him. Nonchalant. In truth, she keenly savoured his musky, masculine scent. The spicy, woody, evocative allure of his aftershave drew her deep into remembered pleasure.

"Right back at you." His gaze captured hers and held tight. There was smug challenge in the dark depths, his lashes lush and bountiful. Really, the man was an Adonis. A damn god from some ancient mythology, as timeless as the earth.

"I never doubted it." Casual indifference, which took a mammoth effort to pull off especially when the point of contact between their hands told a different story.

"Changed your mind yet?"

"No, Your Highness," she said with a totally fake, satisfied smirk. One that communicated a confidence she didn't feel. A smug feminine power she knew from harsh experience came before a fall. A nasty, life-altering fall. No need for the next step. No need at all. She was intimately familiar with it.

"You're impossible," he complained, his jaw rigid with tension.

She wriggled her hands out of his hold and snatched them back as if he'd stolen something dear to her. He had. He'd stolen her sanity. She was crazy, beyond crazy, to entertain even the thought of sex—incredible sex—hard-to-forget sex—nothing-casual-about-it sex. No. Not going to happen.

"You're insane." Out of his mind if he thought she wanted to get up close and personal with him. Again. What harm would it do? The damage was done. The horse had bolted. She'd been there, done that. She yearned for his touch. Why not? Why not find temporary relief from the need that clawed at her insides. Cathartic. No—the demon in her head was persuasive but crazy. The man was obscenely fertile. Contraception didn't stand a chance. She could end up pregnant again and in more dire straits than before. Besides, Aminah was in danger.

Unless Rashid was right and Aminah had been behind this all along. But wouldn't Aminah have let her know? A small voice somewhere deep and dark in her psyche taunted her.

Wasn't she here in Rashid's clutches? Aminah knew Rashid better than she did. She'd know how damned relentless he was when he wanted something. The thought sent a slow shiver cruising down Jemma's spine—he wanted *her*.

"You want me," he murmured, still too close for her liking, his tone cajoling and warm—enticing—like oozy caramel-centred chocolate. It sent a message of indulgence to her body and desire fizzed in her veins. "You wanted me in New York."

His voice was confident. Thank goodness he wasn't privy to how much she'd wanted him. She wanted him still—with every cell, every breath, every wish that sparked in the air between them. He was an arrogant man and no way would she let him know what he did to her.

"You're deluded."

He studied her as if to peel back the layers of her carefully arranged expression. She had more layers than he'd ever know. Layer upon layer of defences, prickly comebacks, and push-away strategies. She'd allowed him to get close, closer than any man before him and look where that had gotten her. No, this was a very bad idea. She didn't need to indulge in this to know she was playing with fire. A fire that was dangerous at best. Attractive, appealing, nurturing even, he would turn on her if she wasn't careful. And she was careful. She would be careful. She would stay careful. For Sami if not for herself.

"*I* was deluded and at the bar, you caught me off guard. I couldn't believe it was you."

"Convenient," he said.

"I changed my mind. Live with it." Her breath was shallow,

and she fought the pheromones dancing in the air.

"Fine. You'll have to live with what might have been." He settled himself back in his seat as if the loss would be hers. Easy-going. Relaxed. He picked up a sheaf of papers and settled into reading. Altogether too accepting. Too dismissive.

She, on the other hand, was riddled with desire. She leaned closer to the air-conditioning vent, willing the slight breeze to cool her overheated system. The sound of his breath-ing—rhythmic, controlled, at ease—mocked every jagged breath she took. Her heartbeat ramped up. And up. Colours were more vibrant. His scent filled her nose with every breath. She closed her eyes to savour it and dropped her head back against the headrest. He was alpha male. Powerful. Tempting. Tasty. Forbidden. A no-go zone. A war zone. Her body was in battle with her head.

"Changed your mind yet?"

The words were a vibration against her skin, and she opened her eyes to find his lips—too close. "No." The word punched through the magnetic force field, her lips throbbing and begging and yearning for his touch.

"The scent of your arousal in these close confines is... distracting," he murmured.

"I apologise, Your Highness." She gulped, her cocky back-at-you, slipping.

His hand shimmied down the side of her face, over her pounding heart to skim the very tight nub of her breast. He eyed her as he might a sweet treat and her heart slammed into her throat. "I wonder if you taste as good as you smell," he enquired, like a wolf licking its lips.

If he wasn't so damned handsome and her body wasn't so brazenly begging please, she'd have swatted him like the pest he was. "You don't remember me, do you?" Her head pressed further into the leather headrest to create space between them and her mind ricocheted to that night long ago when he'd tasted her good and proper... and she'd shamelessly let him.

"Should I?" His expression was one of studied confusion.

Tears welled in her eyes and she cursed herself. Damn. Since Aminah had vanished, she hadn't stopped tearing up at the slightest provocation. The man got under her skin and he was there to stay, whether she liked it or not. Like a damn burr. Or a parasite, burrowing deep into her psyche. She should banish him from her mind, but as much as she wanted to, his touch was always there. His scent. His taste. The feel of him inside her body. Memory was a torturous beast and every night, as soon as she let go of conscious thought, she suffered a relentless, sensory barrage that claimed her body and her heart.

"No," she replied, her smile weak. One night. A long time ago. On the other side of the world. Of course, he didn't remember her. She was out of place. Out of time. Out of context. Besides, she'd taken every effort to ensure he wouldn't remember her. Coloured contacts. Bleached hair. Just because she thought of him every time she glanced at her beautiful, precious daughter didn't mean he thought of her. "We had a fling. A lifetime ago."

"You *are* her, aren't you? The woman I met in Sydney five years ago." His expression, moments ago ablaze with desire, hardened and his gaze cooled. What had burned between them snap-froze, the sensory connection severed. Ice. There was no other word for it. Ice in the desert.

"Yes," she whispered, confused by the sudden chill. Frightened even.

"Why are you here? Why did you befriend my sister?"

Suspicion was back, snaking into his eyes, along with a steely resistance that sapped her womanly power. Jemma felt vulnerable and exposed. Stupid and senseless. Fanciful even. "I thought…" Fear was a pit of vipers in her belly. She couldn't tell him about Sami so what reason did she have for wanting to speak with him?

"You discovered who I was and thought you would milk me for whatever you could get? So why befriend Aminah? Why not contact me directly?" His hand reached for her hair and held it up. "And why hide behind coloured contacts and golden hair?" His gaze bored deeply into hers and her skin quivered with the shock of it. The man of a moment ago was gone. This man was ruthless and cold and as savage as the scenery around them. She struggled to swallow past the knot in her throat. Tension twisted through her body, leaving her wrung out and weak. She'd told him she was married. What did she expect? Open arms? From his perspective, she'd led him into adultery—unknowingly—then disappeared into the night. The irony was that it had been Rashid who was betrothed to someone else at the time, not her. And she had been left holding the baby. Literally. Anger pushed the tight knot out of her throat and the words she needed into the arctic air between them.

"Because you are the sovereign Prince of Zahidah. A fact you omitted from our conversation that night. Not to mention your betrothal. I'm beginning to think the man I met that night was a figment of my own imagination."

"It was sex, Jemma." His voice was razor-sharp, his expression so thunderous she fought the urge to cower. "A one-night stand." He glared at her as if she were Eve herself.

"Such cynicism," she replied, her heart weeping with the

truth in his frank words. He was right. What had possessed her? He'd seemed so nice. So attentive. And he'd made her *feel* so desirable. The hard reality of coping with her father's mental illness—alone—had left her vulnerable. Aching. And he'd made her feel something other than helpless and desolate and alone. He'd made her feel special and connected and empowered.

Until she'd woken up and the tawdry light of dawn had cleared the besotted fog.

On reflection, she hadn't given him a chance of being anything but a one-night stand. Not her best moment and now she had to face the consequences of that decision.

The vehicle tipped in the sand and the see-sawing motion pitched her body forward. She reached out her hand for balance and found the hard muscle of his thigh. Steely strong. Masculine. Heat of a different kind rose like hot lava, sparking and crackling in the frosty air. She snatched her hand back as the vehicle regained traction and forged on.

"You didn't think to mention you were married *before* we had sex?" The fury in his words whipped her like a barbed tail. "You didn't think I had a right to know *before* I committed adultery?"

"*You* didn't mention your betrothal to Fadila," she parried. She had no right to feel the hurt that rose like a suffocating wave, blurring her vision and stealing her breath. Damn it. Get it together. She should tell him the truth, but then how was she to explain about Sami? No. It was better for him to believe she was an adulterous harlot than to risk her baby.

"That was different," he snapped. "We weren't married, and I didn't run off into the night to return to my wife's bed." His words were jagged with furious edges and every one of them lanced like a blade.

"I'm sorry if I hurt you," she said, her chin refusing to surrender to the shame that coursed through her veins. She hadn't left him to return to her husband's bed. There was no husband, but she couldn't tell him that because if she did, he would soon realise whose daughter Sami truly was and she couldn't risk it. "It wasn't like I planned it that way. We were talking. You were a light in the darkness and for that I was grateful."

"You told me your name was Catherine," he said accusingly, his tone cold.

"My first name *is* Catherine, but I never use it. It was my mother's name. I always go by my second name, Jemma."

"So why did you tell me your name was Catherine?"

"Because that night my soul was bare and bleeding on the bar, as I'm sure you remember." She sighed, the tension in her muscles releasing.

His hand gripped the seat with sufficient strength to leave his knuckles white. Her gaze fell to the crimson heart of his ruby crested ring, the hue of ripe pomegranate. He was silent for a long time and she could see the effort it cost him to rein in his temper.

"Yes," he finally replied, "I do remember and now I understand why you took Aminah's death threats so seriously."

"And now I understand why you didn't tell me who you truly were or about Fadila," she whispered, the words wrung from her rational mind and not the part that even now harboured fantasies about the tall, dark, handsome cliché she'd met in a Sydney bar. "You have responsibilities and your people depend on you. A relationship with a woman you met in a bar on the other side of the world was never an option for the Prince of

Zahidah." She watched him for a long moment. "You probably have a politically-correct someone lined up to take Fadila's place." She should have considered that. Relief fought with disappointment. No way would she be his convenient fling again. "Once Aminah is found, I'd like to go back to Australia." Away from Zahidah and its too tempting leader.

"And what of your husband? Is he here in Zahidah? With Sami?"

"No," she replied, befuddled by the web of lies, her mind sifting back over what she'd told him. What had she said? "Sami is with Margie. Her nanny."

"Is he back in Australia?"

He was like a desert dog with a fleshy bone and Jemma felt the tangle of lies tightening around her, squeezing the breath from her lungs. She couldn't confess there was no husband. Had they got a divorce? Were they separated? Was he away on a work project? What would keep them safe? Her eyes dropped to her left hand. She didn't wear a wedding ring and she felt rather than observed Rashid's blistering gaze following hers. Damn.

"We separated. After…" she struggled to lift her gaze to his, the lies burning on her tongue, "…what happened between us." She gazed instead at the streaming sands behind him. "We tried to keep it together, but it didn't…" she took a breath of the eerily still air and forced herself to look at him. "…work out." Her voice squeaked on the last bit and she drowned just a little in the compassion that flashed through the black ice she saw there.

"What about your child? Does Sami see her father? Is he in Australia or Zahidah?"

Jemma struggled to get her words in order. Truly? It was

like purgatory. She had to look the father of her child in the eye and pretend it wasn't so. The truth was on the tip of her tongue—her forked tongue—but this was about Sami and for Sami she would face the flames of hell, forked tongue at the ready.

"No, she doesn't see him, although she sees his sister." A conflagration of shame reddened her cheeks and seared her eyelashes. It was a terrible, terrible sin to keep the existence of his daughter from him. Unforgivable, she chastised herself. Unavoidable she argued back. There was nothing—nothing—she wouldn't do for her child. Sami's well-being was the reason behind every breath she took.

"You *know* what it's like to be brought up with only one parent. To carry the burden of parental responsibility," he murmured, his gaze holding hers, compassion in its depths.

So, he remembered what she'd told him. He knew more about her than any living person. She'd bared herself to him like a sacrificial offering and in return, he'd shared his own struggles. Even now, she felt flayed open before him and vulnerable in a way she fought to disguise. There'd been power in anonymity. And safety. And... comfort. She shifted her gaze to the glare outside. The sun seared the earth, exposing every grain of sand to its lethal scrutiny. The sky stretched blue, so vast, so far. There was nowhere to hide. No place to shelter. No way to avoid the harsh truth. Rashid had a right to know about his daughter and she would have to tell him. She braced her spine and with a deep breath turned her gaze back to his.

"I came to Zahidah to find you, because..."

His gaze was as sharp as a desert hawk. Hell. She couldn't do it. Not yet. Not before she understood why he was forcing Aminah into a marriage she didn't want. It didn't make sense.

Not from the man she'd known. Even now, rightfully angry as he was, she saw compassion and acceptance in his eyes, along with what? Pain?

"I thought we had a connection. I thought…"

"There was more to our soiree than lust?" he offered. "You thought you might like to explore what happened between us?"

"Ah… yes," she agreed, her cheeks heating with the falsehood. She knew she had no place in his future. Immediate or distant. The past was the past. "But when I found out who you were and after I spoke with Aminah, I decided against it."

He observed her, the intensity of his gaze stripping her bare. Never had she met a man who moved her with just a glance. This was like being flailed or aroused with no opportunity to move or sigh or call out. No hope of release. A blissful agony that had her heart enthralled and her breath paralysed. She struggled against the mesmerising power of him and forced herself to stay silent.

"There is no politically correct someone lined up to take Fadila's place," he murmured, and her heart contracted. With what? Relief? She was a fool.

"I think we both know we have unfinished business," he continued, his tone gentle, his gaze a warm caress. "You were so alone that night as you struggled to make the most awful decision and your husband wasn't there for you. I was. Perhaps that means something. I am attracted to you—still, it seems—but I can't offer you marriage or a future. Our worlds are too different. It would never work." There was something in his tone that made her straighten in her seat.

"And I imagine Sheikh Kamil won't be talking marriage either when he learns that Aminah's father is NOT who he thinks it is." Shock tactics, but she was desperate to shift the conversation from dangerous territory. She didn't want to know what it would take for him to consider their business finished. She was finished. Good enough to bed, but not good enough to marry? She wanted no part of it. Urghhhh. She couldn't marry him. Or share his bed. Or tell him about his daughter. Guilt twisted inside her like a blade. But Rashid had a right to know about Aminah's parentage and she could tell him that. Besides, very soon the whole world would know.

"What did you say?" He paused and his scowl deepened.

"Your father is not Aminah's father," she repeated. Her cheeks flushed with heat.

"What wickedness is this? My mother would never betray my father. It's not possible."

"Maybe she didn't want to marry your father any more than Aminah wants to marry Sheikh Kamil," Jemma reasoned. "Maybe she too was forced to marry against her will. Might she not have allowed herself a dalliance with a man she desired?"

"My parents love and respect each other. My mother is not the woman you describe." His body was rigid beside her and radiated heat like the sun off the tinted glass of the window. "You're accusing my mother of adultery? Do you have proof? A paternity test?"

"Yes, of course."

"A paternity test can be faked. Is that what this is about? Extortion?"

"Extortion? Are you insane?" The man had lost his mind.

"If this isn't about extortion, then what?" he demanded, his spine rigid. A muscle ticked in the tight angle of his jaw as if his teeth were jammed together to stop him from reacting. It seemed she was destined to be black to his white. Chalk to his cheese. X to his Y. Best they keep their hands to themselves and their hormones in check.

She could see the battle he fought to control his temper. She got under his skin. Good. Because he got under hers like a bad case of hives.

"Aminah wants to be free of her marital obligation," Jemma replied. Panic zinged in her chest and she considered her options. She could use the book as blackmail now, but then she'd have to confess to its existence and what if he decided to leave her to fry out here. Her attention shifted to the desert that stretched for endless miles around them. But the book would be released soon. He needed to know if he was to have any chance of stopping it. They could hardly negotiate without the time factor, but with Aminah's disappearance, what had seemed so clear now seemed so murky. Nada's well-being was at stake. Aminah's well-being was at stake.

"What are you hiding?" Rashid's voice was a low growl and every hair follicle responded, stretching up, then collapsing back. She wanted to trust him. He'd come to her rescue at the Red Hummingbird and he hadn't even known who she was. Five years ago, he'd made her feel special for the first time in her life. No. She'd learned from a young age, she had to rely on herself.

"It's nothing you need to worry about. I can handle it." Politeness. Cool clarity of thought. That's what she needed. There had to be a solution. She just had to work it out. Calmly. With Rashid this close? Her mind was a scrambled mess. "If Aminah were to expose the truth," she began, her voice trembling with her temerity, "it would neatly release her from her marital obligation." Not so neatly it turned out. Not so neatly at all.

"Aminah would never bring her family into disrepute." He

frowned as he spoke. "Ever. No matter how angry she is."

Wrong. Wrong. Wrong. Maybe he didn't know Aminah as well as he thought he did. And maybe Jemma didn't know Aminah as well as she thought she did either.

"I won't believe what you've said until I have a chance to speak with my mother and find out the truth for myself. If what you say is true, then Aminah's marriage contract is null and void."

"Why did you promise Aminah to the sheikh when your own marriage fell through?" Jemma queried, unable to hold the question back.

Rashid scowled and his frown created deep divots. His silence was long and furious. Her question hung between them like an ancient blade swinging dangerously close to her jugular. His response, when it came, was like the release of a pressure valve, the freeing of an age-old genie.

"I was eighteen when I agreed to the arrangement with Fadila." His gaze captured hers. "My grandfather engineered it before his death. Part of the marriage agreement was the return of lands lost to Kamil's kingdom during my grandfather's reign. Fadila was a child. Only nine years of age. We were to marry when she turned twenty."

"So, this is about your promise to your grandfather?" *That* was why he'd forced Aminah into this arrangement? Not for her good, but for his. "About a piece of land?" The words lodged in her throat. A piece of land was more important to him—to *his* honour—than his sister. "This was not about selecting a man for Aminah who could make her happy, but about what the man could give in exchange?" She almost spat the words. "You bartered your sister's future for a piece of land?"

"Not just a piece of land." He spoke quietly, his eyes pinning hers. "I don't expect you to understand. You were not raised in a royal family. This land is not just important to Zahidah, it is vital for our future. Sometimes what's best for the majority is more important than what's best for the individual. But in this case, marriage to Kamil is a good proposition for Aminah."

"Did you have feelings for Fadila?" She'd touched a raw nerve she could see that. He crossed his arms and his jaw went rigid.

"None I didn't get over." He glared in her direction.

It was like his words had been sharpened and flung from a bow. She took a moment to recapture her calm. This wasn't about her. It was about Aminah. For Aminah, she could be strong. For herself? It hurt. It still hurt.

"Fadila's betrayal was more than twelve months ago," she pointed out. "You don't look like you're over it."

"Fadila waited until our wedding day to defy her father…"

He had been left at the altar. Not literally, but close enough. No. She wouldn't feel sorry for him.

"…What you wouldn't know is that she had a lover. And a pregnancy to hide." His scowl reached new depths and she could see how much he'd hurt.

"Fadila was pregnant?"

His eyes bored into hers, bright with emotion, as if daring her to pity him. Her mind raced and then it came out in a rush. A shocked rush. "She was supposed to be a virgin."

"Yes."

Honour is important in Zahidah. She could see the cost to his pride. He'd been treated badly—*very badly* in his view—by a woman promised to him in good faith. Yet another woman sacrificed at the altar of an arranged marriage to an older man. Desperate enough to take matters into her own hands to avoid it.

Rashid believed Zahidan women had more honour than she did?

She had never done to a man what Fadila had done to him but given the same level of desperation and fear for her future, she could well imagine she might.

And perhaps what Jemma had done was worse. She'd kept her pregnancy from him. Even now, she sat beside him and kept the knowledge of his four-year-old daughter to herself. When Sami hadn't responded to the chemo and a bone marrow transplant had become the treatment of choice, Jemma had been forced to come to Zahidah to find Sami's father. She'd made decisions, desperate decisions, on the run. Her own bone marrow wasn't a match. There wasn't a match on the registry. Aminah had saved Sami's life and there was nothing Jemma wouldn't do to repay her. There was nothing Jemma wouldn't do to protect Sami, even if it meant sitting beside Rashid and keeping the knowledge of his child to herself.

Rashid sat, silent and stoic, tense with pent-up emotion. He too was in a difficult position. "If Fadila's father is the man Aminah is to marry, then what about *his* honour? Surely, he is obligated to repair the injury done to you? Why didn't he just *give* you the land in compensation?"

"The land deed needs to be tied to a marriage contract. It is what his people will accept and understand. If he were to gift the land to the people they have warred with over centuries, there would be great unrest. He will be a good husband for Aminah. He is an honourable man, even if his daughter did the wrong thing. He promised to take care of Aminah. Honour is vital in our culture. If a man's word can't be trusted, he is nothing."

Rashid raked his hands through his hair and the movement tripped her heart. A part of her wanted to take him in her arms and soothe his hurt, but the rest was still riled. Besides, his dark energy and back-off body language told her he didn't want her sympathy.

"Women should not be pawns in your royal games. Aminah is in the same position Fadila was. Trapped."

"You are not a member of the royal family. I don't expect you to understand." He paused before shifting his gaze to the window. "We are headed to the border with Daija. You will see the land for yourself and perhaps then you will understand. There is always unrest in this region—it is a mountainous area and arid. Food and water are scarce. I will mediate talks and keep things from escalating further."

"Why is there unrest?"

"The Daiji and Zahidan people have fought over land and water for centuries. Put your inquisitive mind to rest."

Jemma leaned back in her seat and fell silent, but her mind was far from at rest.

Chapter Eight

The sun was low in the sky by the time they reached their camp for the evening. They were still a day from the border with Daija. The oasis came upon them suddenly, like a mirage in the shimmering glow of orange heat and it took Jemma a full moment to believe her eyes. Palm trees and crystal-clear water, bubbling from a spring beneath the ground. She could see temporary accommodations had been erected. Presumably, Rashid's staff had travelled ahead. Two separate tents, she was relieved to see, although tent seemed too small a word for the glamorous abodes. Rashid was a prince. The truth of it kept ramming itself into her head. His life was a million light years from hers in every direction.

Jemma stepped from the vehicle with considerable relief. She stretched her legs and restrained the urge to run and dive into the water as a wave of heat descended upon her. Instead, she walked to the water's edge, shucked off her slippers and stepped into the shallows. Her toes sank into soft, satiny sand like baby powder beneath her feet. She sighed as she breathed in the spicy scent of dinner roasting and savoured the blissful cool of the water, shaded by the trees. Her gaze greedily appreciated the green after hours and hours of looking at sand. She lifted her camera, taking shot after shot. The desert sky was a flaming pallet in the background and the stretch of sand beyond the trees glowed like it was lit from within.

Rashid walked powerfully towards her, his robes billowing in the wind. He looked so far beyond attractive that every sane thought she had was stolen by the breeze and scattered over the vast sandy plains. She lifted her lens and took a volley of shots, zeroing in on his face. He was majestic. Like a lion surveying the savannah. Rashid smiled at her and she couldn't help but return it. She realised she was happy to be here with him. One day, Sami would know this amazing man was her father and hopefully she would understand why Jemma had made the choices she had.

"I have arranged a bath for you and a cold beverage." His gaze studied her as if to assess her well-being. "I'm sure you must be weary."

"Thank you." Her pulse thumped loudly in her ears. When he looked at her like that, with all of his attention focused on her, with appreciation in his eyes and a hunger that promised all kinds of pleasure… she couldn't think straight, let alone remember why it wasn't a good idea to indulge the crazy wishes that zinged like soda pop in her veins.

"I remember your eyes." His tone was wistful. "They are a turquoise more stunning than the water behind you. Don't hide them from me… anymore."

"No, Your Highness." She was crazy mad at herself for softening. She wanted so much more than he could give.

"And I remember our night together." He said it darkly as if he'd tuned into the direction of her thoughts.

"I'm sure it was nothing out of the ordinary… *for you.*" She cursed when she realised the implication. It had been for her.

"Forgive me if I stopped thinking of you warmly when I

discovered you were the kind of woman who picked up men in bars and had sex behind your husband's back. I'm not often wrong in my assessment of people, but I was blinded when it came to you."

"We were both under a misconception, but it was probably for the best." Her gaze shifted to the flaming sky. "You are a prince and I'm not..." She left the sentence unfinished. Not close to being good enough for a member of the royal family. Not close to being good enough to be the mother of his daughter. It took scarcely a thought to know he'd be disappointed on that front, too. A daughter. Not a son.

"Our night together was very memorable." He took her hands in his.

"Yes," she agreed. Her vision swam with stupid tears as heat and hope shimmied from the point of contact. Really, Jemma? Get it together. She'd been special enough for a night of casual sex. Great sex, really great sex. His fingers meshed with hers. His touch was wickedly delicious and promised a level of care and consideration she didn't deserve. "I might go and have that bath." She pulled her hands from his and turned her attention to the horizon to hide her reaction. "It's so stunningly beautiful here." And quiet, blissfully quiet. It was like they had the place to themselves. His staff was discreet to the point of being invisible.

"Tonight..." His voice was a soft caress. "...we will declare a truce and eat under the stars. We will talk and you will tell me more about yourself. I have many questions."

"Okay." She agreed, for what option did she have? She could hardly say no, thank you. Her thoughts were all over the place and she fought the syrupy surrender in her veins. She couldn't soften. She couldn't let go of her anger. It was the only thing that kept her head clear. While she had a better understanding of why Rashid had treated Aminah the way he had, she was no more in favour of a royal life for Sami. No. It was for the best. She'd made the right decision. She would protect Sami. And if the means were a little clumsy, well, her intentions were golden.

And golden is how she felt after being pampered and blissfully spoilt by a palace attendant. By the time she was dressed for dinner—which felt ridiculously like a date—she was deliciously relaxed. They would eat together because circumstance dictated it. There was nothing more to it than that. She left her feet bare. Her toenails were polished to perfection and her feet had been pampered until they were baby-soft and sweetly scented. The sand beneath her feet was powdery and cool. She followed a makeshift path flanked by tall open-flame torches towards a table with two chairs set close to the water. More torches had been thrust into the sand and a fire pit burned for warmth. The scene was picture-perfect. The moon hung low and heavy in the sky, full and gleaming, its path a glimmering ribbon across the mirror-like surface of the water. The scents in the air made her tummy growl, but she stopped in her tracks when she saw Rashid, statue-still, his back towards her, his face to the distant moon.

Like an ancient warrior. Like time eternal. Like master of the universe. A plethora of stars shone above him, millions and billions spread across the sky in a galaxy of endless horizons. She stood frozen. Her heart beat raw and rapid in her chest. The desert at night was breathtaking. Rashid *and* the desert at night were heart-stopping. She took a deep gulp of the cool night air and pulled her robe closer as if she could protect herself from all that she felt.

She accepted a glass of champagne from a waiter who materialised from the darkness only to step back into the void, invisible and unheard. She sipped as she moved closer to the man who waited... for her. The thought shimmied down her spine and she desperately held on to her defences. Don't let him in. Don't soften. Don't surrender. Not now. Not when she'd come so far. For Sami, for Aminah, for her own sanity, she needed to stay distant.

Rashid was synonymous with the desert and she was under no illusion that he wasn't as dangerous. Steady. Breathe. Each step took her closer, closer to the scene of seduction set before her. He turned and she stopped, captured in the beam of his dark, ebony gaze. Her breath jammed in her lungs. He was majestic. Regal. Proud.

He moved towards her, but she couldn't move. When he reached her, he took her free hand and linked it with his, drawing her closer to the table. There was music. She hadn't noticed that before, too enthralled by the whole. Soft, sensual music. He lowered her glass to the table and took her into his arms. She moved towards him with a synchrony as seamless as the stars and the moon. Their bodies knew each other intimately. She knew his rhythm. His soul.

"What do you think of the desert at night?" She could hear it in his voice. Pride. As if the heavens belonged to him alone. As if the desert sky was his to share at will.

"It's breathtaking," she managed, through vocal cords tight with emotion. Rashid was proud. She could see that now. Proud of his heritage. Proud of his country.

"I'm glad I can share it with you."

Her hair had been whipped into a princess-style hair creation. Jewels rested on her forehead in a head circling adornment and the smooth silk of her gown was a sensual caress against her skin. She felt like a princess tonight. Rashid's face was smooth against hers and he smelt clean and spicy and musky. She breathed him in, savouring their closeness, assuring herself it was just for a moment. A heady, self-indulgent moment. Like a sensory photograph. A moment to remember. A snapshot in time.

"You're beautiful, Jemma." He tilted her face to his, his hand gentle under her chin. "Your eyes are just as I remember them." She felt exposed. Vulnerable. Why hadn't she ignored his arrogant command? She'd learned to hide behind the vibrant colours in her eyes.

"Thank you." Her body still sung with the pleasure of scented oils and the kneading of her tired muscles. "I was very well looked after."

"You didn't complain once about the pitching of the vehicle," he murmured, his gaze soft. "It can be tiring. Frightening even."

Stay strong. He doesn't really care. It's just politeness. "I'm tougher than you think, Your Highness," she whispered, her voice losing traction as he pulled her closer. Damn. The intensity of his focus left her wanting things she shouldn't. Like his touch. Like his kiss. Like his skin against hers. He lifted his hand to her face and rested his palm against the plane of her jaw. She melted, literally, from the inside out like a marshmallow held to one of the dancing flames. With a will of its own, her hand curled around his neck and into the silk of his hair. Their bodies were close, so close she felt him hard against her and her body swirled with a thousand wishes.

Rashid's arms tightened around her and she felt safe and cherished and treasured and... what was she thinking? She wasn't thinking. She was feeling. And his mouth was against hers, coaxing her to open to him, promising all kinds of wonderful. And then the stars shattered as he tasted and supped and savoured, and she met him with equal tenacity, taking as much as giving, giving as much as taking, lost to time and space and any kind of sanity because this was pure craziness. Madness. Addiction. What raced in her veins was more potent than any drug, more demanding, more crucial. She tasted like he was her last meal. Like he was her last breath. Like her world began and finished with the stroke of his tongue against hers and the magic he conjured. She clung to him, physically wrapped herself against him with no regard to her pride, her body clamouring to join his. Mindless, formless desire. It unfurled inside her like the proverbial serpent.

When he set her aside, when he invited the cool night air between them, she openly grieved his touch.

"Dinner, Thameen."

"Oh. Yes. Of course." She was mad at herself. What was wrong with her? Had she learned nothing?

"You taste as good as I remember," he said, his hand warm on the small of her back as he steered her towards the table and the steaming bowls of food. Lashings of roasted alfaham chicken, baba ghanoush, pickled olives and tabouleh salad.

Jemma settled into her seat and sipped her champagne, her gaze shifting to the magnificence of the night sky and its reflection on the inky black water. The air was still, and the fire burned warm in the pit not far away, crackling and shooting sparks into the air. Her pulse thudded in her ears. She turned her attention back to the man opposite her, resplendent in the traditional dress of the desert, his eyes as dark and savagely beautiful as the scenery around her.

Keep it together, Jemma. He's a prince. A desert prince. You're a nobody. He has all the power and you have none.

"Help yourself, Thameen." He gestured to the platters on the table and she didn't need to be asked twice. She was hungry and the food looked amazing.

"Thank you."

He watched as she took a good serving of everything and after she tasted it, she moaned her appreciation. "Mmmmm. This is amazing. Thank you."

"Your thanks should be given to the chef, I think," he said with a smile.

"Yes, you're right. I must thank him. I'm looking forward to sleeping here. In Australia, we call this glamping."

"Glamping? I've not heard of that word." His eyebrows lifted, the light from the open flame torches dancing across his face.

"Glamourous camping. An indulgent camping experience. The best kind, from my perspective, although this takes glamour to a whole new level. And my bath?" Words defied how good that had been. "Pure indulgence."

"I'm glad you enjoyed it."

She turned her attention to her meal and their conversation was effortless and relaxed. He drew her into various topics, and she reciprocated until they sat back, well-sated, the dishes removed from the table and a pot of coffee resting between them. He took a sip of the strong, thick brew from a small cup. "Now," he said. "Tell me about your childhood. What do you remember of Zahidah?"

"I remember the desert, the vast sky, and camping out with my father. Not like this. Sleeping bags beside a fire, I think. I don't really have memories beyond that. Patchy ones. My favourite ice cream. The feel of the sand stinging my legs in the wind. The smells of spices. I was young when we left here, and we moved a lot. My father was a photographer and a painter. A bit of a bohemian."

"It must have been difficult to develop friendships if you were constantly moving from one place to another," he mused.

"Yes." Jemma was surprised by his insightfulness. "But my father needed me. He wasn't very good at practical things like washing or shopping or cooking."

"Ah, that explains it. You appear well used to looking after yourself. What about your mother? You said she and your brother died in Zahidah? How old were you?"

Grief snapped at the edge of her awareness like it always did when she thought of her mother. She'd learned to hold it at bay. There was a space she'd found not unlike this oasis, where she could escape. Her emotions prowled at the edges, but it was a sanctuary of sorts where she could breathe like everyone else without the risk of feeling too much. This man took her to the very edge, and she teetered there, unwilling to venture into the darkness. "My mother died soon after my birth. My twin brother with her."

"Your father had to cope with a new baby on his own whilst grieving for the rest of his family?"

"Yes." Emotion snaked into her throat and unfurled to block her breath.

"Do you look like your mother?"

His questions were relentless.

"My father thought so." She paused not wanting to give too much away. "He found that difficult." She kept her gaze on the fire as if she could shield herself from his prying attention. "He never really recovered from his loss. He struggled with depression. There were women, but none

111

who stuck." He'd moved from one woman to another with monotonous regularity and she'd learned from a young age that she'd rather be the leaver than the leavee. She tried to hold it in, but Rashid's compassion and the wine and the warm fire and the cocoon of care he created had her wanting to share.

"I used to worry…" She forced back the memories. "I used to come home from school and… there were times when I'd find him unconscious, an empty medicine bottle beside him. I'd call an ambulance and they'd keep him alive, but he never thanked me. His mood waxed and waned over the years. Some days he'd be fine, others not so much." Ultimately, she'd failed. The thought was a dagger to her heart. Without a care, he'd left her alone in the world to fend for herself. It was what she was used to, she reminded herself. She was capable, more than capable of looking after herself.

Rashid's gaze held hers. "You couldn't save him. You told me that when we met in Sydney."

"No." She shook her head, her vision blurred by a veil of tears. Her emotions were a knot in her throat. The agony she'd held so tight inside her began to unravel. Just a notch.

"You're not alone. Not anymore." He took her hands in his, the warmth of his palms encompassing hers. "And we'll find Aminah. She is more resilient than you think."

"When Aminah told me she'd rather die than marry Sheikh Kamil, I had to do something. I couldn't stand by and let her…" Tears spilled onto her cheeks. Hell. Now? What was wrong with her? For years, she hadn't cried. But since Sami's illness? Sobs. Too big to hold in. Rashid came to her side and enclosed her in the warmth of his embrace. She held onto the solid muscle, the steely strength she sensed there. Held on while emotions buffeted her with every snatched breath. "Aminah asked me to help her. I couldn't…"

Rashid held her, strong and sure, until her breath came easier.

"Not help," she finished on a stifled sob.

"Aminah was wrong to manipulate you." He passed her some tissues and she gratefully used them to tidy her face. He stepped away, but his hand stayed with hers as he sat down opposite her, their fingers loosely linked. He reached for the pot to refresh their coffee. "Aminah is very good at getting what she wants. The role of junior wife to Sheikh Kamil comes with little cost and great privilege. What made you think to have a paternity test done?"

"Her blood type is B, which is not common. When she mentioned her parents were both O positive, it was worth exploring."

"I'm O positive," he reflected, tension in the tight line of his jaw. "I will speak with my mother."

"A woman's choice of partner should be her own," Jemma persisted. "No woman should be forced to marry a man old enough to be her grandfather."

"Aminah is a princess. Her life is not her own. There are expectations. Demands. But there are also rewards." Rashid's tone was scathing.

"Aminah didn't feel that way. She was desperate to escape. Perhaps your mother was, too."

"Aminah wanted what you take for granted. Your independence and freedom to do as you please. But she has a family. Being part of a family brings the need for compromise. Being part of a royal family brings responsibility. She took advantage of your empathy and allowed you to take responsibility for her problem."

"I disagree. She was fully prepared to take whatever measure was necessary to avoid this marriage." Jemma admired her tenacity. "A woman should have a right to choose who she shares her body with. To be forced to spend every night with a man she finds repugnant is a form of prostitution."

"And you rushed to her rescue. The same way you have for your father over the years." His fingers moved softly against hers, soothing, comforting.

"Yes. She felt alone. Afraid." Better to provoke him than to succumb to the spell he cast with his kindness and compassion, but he didn't react. Not for a moment. Her hand remained in the harbour of his, not banished. Not yet.

"You must miss your father."

"Yes," she agreed, stifling the rising flood of emotion with another sip of her drink. "But I have my work and my daughter."

"What do you do?"

"I'm a writer and a photojournalist. I speak with amazing people and give a voice to those who can't speak for themselves. When I was younger, my father and I travelled a lot. I didn't need anyone, I relied on myself." And she'd liked it that way. Or at least she had until Sami had come into her life. Now her focus was on creating what was best for Sami,

"Ah, now I understand the camera." He paused and considered her for a long moment. "You have everything Aminah thinks she wants."

"You may be right," Jemma agreed. "But Aminah has a family who loves her and that's worth more." Thanks to Rashid, Jemma had Sami. Sami was her everything and Aminah was the shiny, glacè cherry on top. She was grateful for what she had. She didn't need anything more.

"Aminah may have sought to protect you," he said gently.

"This may be *her* plan unfolding. One she didn't share with you."

"No. Aminah wouldn't do that. We planned to travel together."

Could Rashid be right? Aminah had the documents they'd worked to obtain. She could have left the country, and no one would know. Jemma was the only one who knew her identity. If the book was released—any day now—the royalties would go into Aminah's account. It was feasible. She could have done it. But she wouldn't. She would know that Jemma would worry. No. Aminah wouldn't do that. Not even to protect her. Jemma was sure someone else was behind it. Someone who didn't want the landholding passed back to Zahidah. It was too much of a coincidence.

"Was the man Fadila eloped with a Daiji?"

"No, Jemma," he growled, his expression carefully controlled.

"He could have been paid off by the Daiji. Her elopement put a stop to your marriage and now Aminah has disappeared. A bit of a coincidence, don't you think? The Daiji people have the most to gain if the marriage doesn't go ahead. The most to lose if it does. They could have taken matters into their own hands. Why would they give up the land their ancestors died to acquire?"

"I don't believe there was a conspiracy." His dark expression thundered. "The land belongs to Zahidah. It was lost in my Grandfather's time, but before that it was ours for eons. The tribal leaders have no choice but to accept the terms of Kamil's agreement. They are honour-bound to follow the dictates of the reigning sheikhdom."

"That doesn't mean they'll do it blithely," she argued.

"Nor does it mean they'd kidnap a princess to stall the

proceedings." His fingertips pressed into his forehead as if his worries had collected there and caused him pain.

"They're Bedouin. Their community is remote from the city. Their honour code may be different from yours."

"Kidnapping a princess is punishable by death. There has been no ransom demand. There is no reason to think Aminah is caught up in the tensions there."

"Then it's imperative they keep her hidden. *If she's there*," Jemma said with hope in her heart. "I could wander the camp and listen to the talk. Maybe somebody will know something."

"I can't search the Daiji camp without some kind of evidence she's there."

"Why not? They are the ones most likely to be involved."

"I will speak with the Daiji leader. If there's any reason to suspect they are hiding her, I'll know." He reached for his cup and took a long draught, his scowl deepening. "My security staff are working on this. If there is any reason to suspect the Daiji, they will advise me."

Jemma took a deep breath and allowed herself to be cajoled into silence, but the more she thought about it, the more it made sense. The Daiji people had the most to lose if Aminah's marriage went ahead. There was political unrest in the region. Wasn't that why they were heading there? She sipped her coffee and eyed the man across from her. "What about you?" she asked. "Did your father bring you out into the desert?"

"My grandfather did. We came out here many times. We would sit together by the fire and he would tell me stories about those who came before him. I always knew what my life would be like. There was a master plan and I was an important part of it."

"Was it good to know what your future held? Or did you

want to rebel and create your own?" She watched the dance of emotions over his face, the shadows that moved in his eyes.

"There were times when I wanted to be a regular person. Being part of the royal family comes with great privilege but also great burden. At times, I resented the duty I was beholden to. It was liberating to spend the night with a woman who didn't know who I was. I had the freedom to be myself and I thank you for that. It was a blissful escape." He held her gaze with his and his fingers were there, warm and snug around hers, his words like warm chocolate to her soul.

"I have learned that most things come at a price," he finished. "The cost of our night together was real enough, but it did not diminish the pleasure of my dreams."

She shivered as a cold breeze climbed her spine. Their night together *had* come at a price; a far greater price than he could know. It was eerie that he should mention dreams. She suffered endless dreams of him as if her subconscious wanted what her conscious brain couldn't have. Perhaps it was the same for him.

"Tell me about Sami," he continued.

"She's four now and very strong-willed." Like her father, she thought as she observed the steady intensity of his gaze. "Which is fortunate, or she wouldn't have survived." Her heart squeezed with fear and relief and love. She would tell Rashid as much as she could of his daughter without throwing Sami to the wolves. Well, to one wolf in particular. He gazed at her with a salacious light in his eye as if he'd like to unwrap and devour her. She pulled her clothing tighter across her chest and braced her spine.

"Sami was diagnosed with acute lymphoblastic leukaemia when she was two years of age. The chemotherapy was horrendous, and it didn't work. The doctors increased the dose but there was no sign of a response. I was told she needed a bone marrow transplant, but I wasn't a match." Rashid's grip on her hands tightened, his fingers linking with hers, and the knot inside her unravelled another notch as warmth seeped into her soul. He was too intelligent not to ask the questions that would lead to the answers she didn't want to give.

"And you found a match in Zahidah?"

"Yes, we did and now Sami is recuperating. She is six months post-transplant and the signs are very positive that she will be completely cured. We were given the all-clear to travel home a week before Aminah disappeared."

"And you met Aminah at the hospital while Sami was undergoing treatment?"

She hesitated a moment. They had met Aminah at the hospital, but only after Jemma had gone to great lengths to ensure their paths crossed so she could ask the question Sami's life depended on. "Yes, Aminah has been a great comfort to us. Without her, Sami would not have recovered as well as she has." Without Aminah, Jemma would have been forced to ask Rashid to be tested, and Sami's life would have been at risk in other ways. There was no doubt she owed Sami's life to the selfless woman who came to their rescue without a moment's hesitation. "Your sister is very special to me."

"Yes, I see." He considered her for a long moment as if privy to the hidden meaning behind her words, which of course he wasn't. "You must be tired. Shall we retire for the evening?"

"Yes." Jemma moved to extract her hands from the shelter of his. His grip tightened and she lifted her gaze to his.

"You've been through so much." His gaze was intense in the firelight, his touch provocative. Jemma quivered from the inside out. "You're an amazingly brave and capable woman, but you're not alone. Not now. Not tonight… unless you want to be."

"Thank you." Her voice was a whisper as if the words she needed were raw and unpalatable and difficult to say. "But no. That would be unwise." The man of her dreams was looking at her as if she was a most precious treasure. He could have anything he wanted, anything… and he wanted her. What she wanted more than anything was what she saw in his eyes. The promise of her every wish fulfilled. The promise of pleasure. Of pure indulgence. She didn't need to go there to know just how good his promises were or just how well he lived up to them.

"No, you're probably right."

There was magic between them and it drew her towards him, or maybe he still had her hands and he'd yanked her off centre, she really couldn't be sure, but she found herself caught in a force she couldn't deny. Before she could whisper no from her yearning, parting lips, his were there, on hers and she was lost in a kiss more heart-breaking than any she'd known. Tender, yes, and appreciative, like she was the most beautiful woman in the world. Hungry, like she was the only one who could ease the ache inside him. Slow, like they had all the time in the world, and magnetic, like she had no choice but to get closer, to savour the scent of his skin, to become lost in his taste, his promises, his wishes.

And for the longest time, she let them master her, until the words that pounded in her temple like waves from a distant shore grew louder. She couldn't do this. She shouldn't do this. Not without telling him about Sami and there it was, the guilt that twisted inside her like a rusted blade. She drew back from the abyss.

"I need to go," she murmured, her toes curling in the soft, silky sand.

"Are you sure?" His lips were close to hers and she felt rather than heard his words, his breath a heady temptation that coaxed her to let go, to stop fighting, to just give in to the sensations that eddied through every part of her body; and truly, the strength had long gone from every muscle.

"Yes." The words were prised from her lips by the same nasty blade that hacked through her wishes and her dreams and exposed her for what she was. The mother of his child. A child he didn't know he had. She had no right to feel cherished and loved and adored by this man. He would hate her for what she'd done. What she'd done was unforgivable. There was no way forward for them. This was a mistake. "I need to go. This isn't right. Not with Aminah missing and..."

"I'll walk you to your door." He took her hand in his and steered her along the torch-lit path.

"Thank you." The traitor inside her stirred uncomfortably. She wanted what he wanted. She wanted what he offered with every breath and she fought her desire, tooth and nail. Not. Going. To. Happen.

Chapter Nine

J emma's proximity was a hell to be endured. Here, in the close confines of the vehicle, her sweet scent filled his head. Every breath was torture. So much for *her* death-by-desert sentence. Ironically, it was *he* who was dying one agonising breath at a time.

"When will we arrive?" Jemma asked.

"Soon." Thank the heavens. He'd kept his hands to himself, but he wanted—he wanted—and then some. His companion was an intoxicating minx and her snappy mouth was as much a thrill to him as her sleek, sexy body. He enjoyed her company. She challenged him. She bristled with intelligence. She soothed, provoked, cajoled, entertained and she didn't talk incessantly. Their silences were comfortable… fortifying.

He captured the turquoise of her eyes, more beautiful than the finest gem, and pondered the connection he found there. She wanted him as much as he wanted her, he was sure of it. Every moment in her company spurred him to take control, but she was so damn contrary she fought him every step of the way. Her surrender—her willing surrender—had become more important to him than his next breath.

"Our hosts will assume you're my *Habibti* and I'm disinclined to advise them otherwise." He observed the flare in her pupils.

She fought herself. Still. It was there in the fleeting crease that crossed her brow. Her scent was intoxicating, alluring. Images from their night in Sydney came back to haunt him; her beautiful hair, a curtain of auburn silk against the darker tone of his torso as she explored him with her mouth.

Being cooped up in this damn vehicle with Jemma was driving him to madness. He didn't want to think of the past. He didn't want to indulge in fantasies that even now, drove him to purgatory night after night.

"You will incite a battle royale if we don't give the clear message that you belong to me." He waited while she processed the implications of his words. "It is for your safety, but it would mean sharing accommodations."

He watched her reaction. The press of her teeth into the soft lushness of her lower lip sent an answering leap to his groin. In her company, there'd been no respite from the aching need that simmered in his body. From dormant and dead to the world of women, she'd woken within him a rapacious appetite. Determination settled in the fine lines of her forehead and he prayed she'd see things his way.

He turned his gaze to the window and gave no outward sign that her response made a hoot of difference to him. It took his full concentration to ease the path of his breath, to fight the snags that threatened to give him away. His heart beat a loud percussion in his ears, and he focused on the sliding sand outside the window. He wouldn't let this opportunity slip away. He couldn't. He wanted her. To hell with expectations and royal duty. He wanted to lose himself in her ripe womanly centre and forget the agony of wanting a woman he couldn't have.

"Perhaps a united front is best," she said slowly, "but are you gentleman enough to keep your hands to yourself?"

"You don't like to let anyone close."

"No, Your Highness."

His insides clenched with her mocking barb. He threatened her. He could see it. She prickled and defended and built walls a mile high. She was afraid. Afraid he'd see her. Afraid he'd want more than she was able to give? The feeling was mutual. He had nothing to give. Nothing he hadn't lost five years ago when he'd fallen for a woman who belonged to another man. Nothing he hadn't lost after Fadila's betrayal. If she could see him on the inside, she'd see a landscape that was charred. Dead. Empty. Hollow. There was no danger their hearts would get in the way of their attraction. The list of cons was endless.

"I'd really like to ease this relentless physical ache."

"I feel it, too. As much as I don't want to." Her honesty was pure. A different kind of virtue, but worth a lot to a man who had been deceived and lied to. She endlessly surprised him.

"Then let's do something about it. Defuse it. Extinguish it." He could think of nothing else. She made him wait. Not one minute. Not two. A full fifteen minutes of nerve-grating silence. If she wanted him to beg, well damn it, he'd beg.

"Fine." She crossed her arms and looked away from him.

Pig-headed, obstructive, provocative witch. He couldn't see her expression or the nuances in her eyes, but her body sang with tension.

"Fine, what?"

"Fine. Let's scratch the damn itch and get it over with." Her eyes swung back to his, ferocious and scathing.

"That's not what I had in mind."

Cocky bluster was her way of hiding. He could see the shadows behind the challenge, the vulnerability she fought to disguise. Even now as her chin jutted out and she eyed him like a praying mantis might eye its mate, he inwardly chuckled. She challenged him at every step. He knew exactly where he stood with her. Her shadows and complexities were fascinating, and he yearned to peel the layers back. To find out what made her so self-sufficient and determined to keep the world at bay.

"I had in mind a slower savouring of sensation." He reached over and took her hand in his. "Starting now." He lifted her hand to his mouth and lavished her palm with his attention. His gaze clung to hers.

She looked startled. Her pupils flared at just the heat of his breath. Oh, he couldn't wait to explore further. He kissed her palm for a long worshipping moment.

She snatched her hand back and scowled at him.

"I'm more of a race-to-the-finish kind of girl. There's no need for the early start."

He lifted his brows as if to say: I see you. I see what you do. She used shock tactics to leave others off-centre. Disarmed. Not him. Not anymore. The desert didn't move at the pace of the city. Here, a slower hand was required.

Sitting back, he tempered the satisfied grin that spread upwards from his chest. She could fight all she liked, but tonight when she came to his bed—willingly—he would teach her about intimacy. He would love her body thoroughly. With very close attention to detail.

No racing for the finish line. Until he'd taken his fill of her, he could think of nothing else.

Bands of horsemen swooped down on their vehicle, whooping wildly, rifles firing into the sky, plumes of sand and dust billowing out from the horses' hooves. Jemma reached for Rashid's hand, fearing they were being set upon. Her heart leapt with every erratic lurch of the vehicle. Rashid's grip encompassed hers, the heat banishing the chill that slowed the blood in her veins.

"It's alright, my Habibti. They've come to welcome us."

The muscular beasts wheeled around and galloped alongside, their riders resplendent in bright and colourful robes, their saddle hangings decorative. Camel men appeared and by the time they drew into the tented community, they were quite the cavalcade. Long, wavering, high pitched wails came to her ears as the vehicle slowed to a stop.

Rashid stayed her, his gaze intense. "Wait here."

He opened the door and stepped out to a ceremonial welcome. She saw the wielding of a curved dagger, the splash of blood as the blade plunged into the throat of a pure white camel. These were a people who would sacrifice their last meal for a stranger. For their prince? She shuddered. Their customs had not softened with the passing years.

When the slaughter was done, Rashid reached into the vehicle to draw her out. Care, consideration, and compassion were there in his gaze and stirred her like a heated caress. He'd sought to protect her from the gruesome sight. One that even now scarred the inside of her eyelids.

Red hot heat struck her face like a slap. She lowered her head with respect to the tribal elders. It was late afternoon, but the force of the sun was brutal, and the air was so hot her lungs protested as she drew breath. Rashid's grip tightened around her hand, his touch blistering. His careful attention harried her senses until she remembered this was an act. She was his Habibti. His reverent treatment was for the benefit of those watching.

She stayed the foolish fluttering of her heart and lifted her chin to meet the curious, sun-beaten faces of his people with confidence. It was a cocky sham born in defiance. She couldn't care less about their opinion of her. She had nothing to prove. The smell of roasting meat assaulted her nose and her hearing echoed with the ear-splitting sound of the women.

As they moved away from the vehicle toward the tents, her gaze shifted to the rugged, inhospitable terrain. Mountainous rock formations rose from the sand and salt scrub like ancient monuments scattered by the hand of their creator. Behind them, the sky stretched blue into the hazy distance and the lowering sun created shadowy ripples across the sea of sand. The photographer in her yearned to capture it on film.

Was Aminah near? This was the border between Zahidah and Daija. There were no lines to demarcate the boundary. The terrain had risen for most of the day. Several times their vehicle had become stuck in the mountainous dunes.

Here, water was as lucrative as oil.

The crowd parted as Rashid drew her towards a group of elderly men flanked by rough-looking warriors. She was glad for the tenacious hold of his hand around hers. He was a prince. Powerful. Important. A leader of men. He oozed authority and alpha dominance. He was a magnificent man. A lion. A predator.

She desired him. With every cell. She yearned for his possession, but her head screamed caution. To want him was dangerous. To covet such a man was insanity. He would demand total surrender. She sensed it in the possessive grip of his hand, in the rippling muscle and determined stride. She moved in his wake until Rashid released his grip to accept coffee and lower himself onto an elaborate carpet. She was gently drawn away by a bevy of women. His eyes connected with hers, his chiselled mouth lifting at the corners, his gaze scorching. Oh yes, there was promise there. Promise that when he came to her, she would be his. In every way. Her senses scrambled.

What had she done?

Icy apprehension scuttled along her spine as she followed the women to a *buryuut hajar*, a large tent divided into parts by exotic curtains. Rich, colourful mats covered the floor. A rose oil bath awaited her, cool and luxurious. The women served her water and a thick, gritty kind of coffee she sipped more out of manners than a desire to consume.

After a long indulgent soak, she was dried with careful attention to her modesty. Sweet smelling oils were rubbed into her skin and the strong, masterful kneading was a welcome relief to muscles sore from two days of stress and tension in Rashid's company. She listened as the women spoke of their menfolk, their children. By the time they were finished, she felt like a bride on her wedding day. Buffed, polished and scented. A sweet oasis. A man's paradise. Was this what she wanted? Her body screamed yes. The anticipation of Rashid's possession was an erotic burr to be endured. She was drawn from her heavenly retreat to join her hosts.

A feast awaited. Roasted whole sheep nestled in mounds of rice and pine nuts, all drenched in a rich white sauce of yoghurt and butter. With gracious thanks, she took her meal under the majestic theatre of the sunset and darkening sky. Was Aminah close by? The thought distracted her almost as much as Rashid's careful attention. His eyes rarely veered from her except to pay homage to the ceremonial dancers. The temperature dropped with the sun offering blissful relief after the cruel heat of the day.

Jemma struggled to contain the furious gallop of her heart.

The evening drew into night and she excused herself, leaving Rashid deep in conversation with the elders. Would he discover anything about Aminah? Again, she was accompanied by a small group of women who assisted her with her toilette. She wasn't used to such close attention. Her Zahidan wasn't fluent enough to allow normal conversation, but her understanding of their chatter was excellent. Perhaps they assumed her understanding was as poor as her speech because their talk veered to more sensitive matters.

"Layla says Husam has fallen for his beautiful captive." The woman's voice dropped as if there may be ears about other than Jemma's dumb ones and she couldn't catch it. She longed to ask. To break into the conversation, but she feared if she did, she would lose her advantage. Jemma's blood pressure spiked and the force of the blood in her veins near deafened her.

"Husam?" the other woman rejoined and they both laughed.

Who was Layla? Husam? Daijis? Jemma held her breath. The moment was so important she daren't move lest the women stop speaking, but their conversation veered away from what she needed to know. She longed to ask. Did she dare? Would she blow her cover?

She would have to speak in Zahidan. She struggled to find the words she needed.

"Who is Layla?" Stilted, but understandable.

"You speak Zahidan? We thought you were English."

"I speak some," she replied, not wanting to lose her advantage.

"But you understood?"

"Enough. Yes."

The girls squirmed and looked at each other through lowered lashes. "Layla is Husam's attendant. A friend."

"Who is Husam?"

"Husam is the Daiji Imam's son."

"Could he know anything about Princess Aminah's where-abouts?"

"Please, Miss, shh." They glanced behind them with anxious expressions.

Jemma nodded. She could see she'd put them in an awkward position. But then, they'd been speaking over her head as if she were witless. "Your friend, I would like to speak with her."

"It was just talk. Nothing more than whispers."

"She may know something about Aminah. I need to speak with her. I could dress like a servant. Cover my face.

"Your eye colour would give you away. The Daiji people keep to themselves, but we sometimes speak with the women at the waterhole when we wash our clothes."

"What do you suggest?"

The two girls looked at each other. "You could come with us. Perhaps speak to Layla there. Listen to the talk."

"That might work." Jemma pondered the problem. "Will you come for me tomorrow?"

The girls nodded and backed away. She'd clearly frightened them. They were replaced by a young woman with a large fan in her hands. She clearly intended to fan Jemma as she rested.

Jemma tried to stay awake until Rashid could join her. The lantern light flickered and danced, and she watched the long shadows shift on the rich brocade of the curtains at the head of the bed. Lighter, transparent curtains were drawn back on one side. The space was an exotic indulgence and with the cool breeze from the fan and her body's divine pampering, her eyelids drifted closed. She was in the desert. In the mountains. She would find Aminah. Maybe tomorrow. And tonight, when Rashid came to join her? She'd put guilt to the side and find relief. Get him out of her system and put the longing back in perspective.

Rashid ached. With fatigue. With desire. With lust. The talks had gone late into the night and he'd struggled to focus his attention. In the end, he'd called a halt. The remainder would have to wait. The needs of his body could no longer be ignored.

Jemma lay in his bed, her hair tousled and tangled against the darkness of the pillow. Her body was half covered by a sheet, but the fine strap of her ivory nightdress had dropped from her shoulder and lured him closer. The candlelight created intriguing shadows over the porcelain perfection of her skin. Even in sleep, she bewitched him.

He stepped out of his clothing, swollen with need. He was determined to do this his way—not hers. No, the kind of sex that was over in an explosive moment was not what he had in mind. Although that kind of sex had its place. Just not here. Not now. Not with this woman.

He settled himself beside her, stroking her hair back from her face and watched mesmerised as her eyes drifted open. Aquamarine eyes as clear as the sea on a sunny day, fast blotted by her dilating pupils, the growing splash of desire. He stroked the petal soft skin of her cheek, ran his finger along the gentle ridge of her nose to linger on the velvety softness of her lips.

"You must be tired." Her voice was husky with sleep. Under his touch, her body hummed with the same tension that racked his.

"I was." Desire arced between them and he waited, watched

as she fought her way from sleep to wakefulness to arousal.

"I tried to wait…"

He watched her battle to master her defences. Her emotions were there on her face. Her attraction. Her desire for him, yes. But more. He could see the vulnerability she hid behind that veneer of strength and independence. It shot like an arrow to that part of him that was pained and alone. He yearned to hold her, to comfort her and cherish her. He would pleasure her like no other man had. She would learn that intimacy was a delicious thing to be savoured, not rushed.

"I want you," he muttered. She had no idea how much. He closed his arms around her, and she rolled onto him, her lips close, so close to his, her hair cascading around him.

"I want you, too." She offered the words like a gift to his mouth and he drank them in. Drank of her scent—the elixir of her breath—knowing she needed to take the reins, to feel in control. Her fears ran deep. They raced there in the depths of her eyes. Darker now, more stormy. He waited, his lips craving the intimate ecstasy of hers yet still she hovered above him. Her intoxicating spell ensnared him. Enthralled him. The heat of her lithe body on top of his fuelled a tempest of desire he fought to restrain, to rein in, to control.

"Your Highness, I want to kiss you." Her smile was provocative, her breath tantalising and sweet.

"What happened to Raz?"

"It turned out Raz wasn't real." He could see the emotion, the raw intensity in her eyes. Desire, yes, but something more.

"Oh, he's real alright and hungry for you," he countered.

"Pheromones. Attraction," she whispered, as if to define the boundaries.

"Yes." He fought for breath, his lungs tight, his head fit to rage. "Jemma, kiss me or I swear I won't be responsible for what I do." She was a witch. She had him in a sensual spell, enraptured, desperate for one taste, one touch, one kiss. He could see what she wanted. She wanted him to lose control. To take what she offered with greedy rapaciousness. Not. Going. To. Happen. The words ignited in his head, loud and furious. He could do this. He could take her to a place she hadn't been before. He would have his sensual way with her. Break down her defences. Why her surrender had become so important, he didn't know. Perhaps it was because Jemma was a challenge... in capital letters. Or perhaps it was because he wanted her to know what it was like to be respected as a woman. He would respect her. He wouldn't rush this.

Breathe.

Her lips closed the miniscule distance and pressed into his with provocative allure, as if to experiment, to tantalise, to taste. Her tongue ran over the ridge of his top lip. Anticipation plunged through him with talons of fire. He rolled her over, took her mouth in a hungry tasting. Hers opened in surprise. Enough for him to invade the honeyed sweetness and stoke a sensual storm that stole his sanity, that took him to the edge of mindful control—he teetered and fought the temptation to plunge into the hell-fires that burned between them and find relief. She dared him. Her body fused with his, her hands pressed close, her nails a delicious provocation. She wanted him. She was ready for him. She wanted him to rush. *He* wanted to rush. His hands greedily travelled the satiny Nevada of her skin. Her scent lured him closer. Her mouth locked to his with bruising need. A demand that cindered his resistance; that ravaged and razed.

Somewhere in the recesses of his rational mind, he found the ruthless determination to rein it in. To drag them both back from the raging heat, the hunger, the tempest of longing. But he didn't break the kiss. He deepened it, softened it, layered it with his need to cherish the moment, to bask in the drugging intensity of it. He allowed his hands to explore the womanly landscape of her body. To touch every curve, every tempting dip. Long, unhurried, languid strokes. He inwardly smiled as the tension eased in her muscles, as her fiery, evocative movements lulled into lolling pleasure.

The kiss moved into deeper, quieter waters.

A place where he touched with reverence. Her face. Her neck. His hands tangled in the heavenly bliss of her hair. Her hands. His kiss was loaded with the promise of passion leashed. Of intimacy. Mesmerizing, simmering desire. The fires were there, he could feel the heat, but here, time didn't exist. He savoured every sigh. Every groan. Every muted sob. The magic they spun together. Their tongues no longer duelled but savoured and ventured closer. His kiss was a thorough, careful, provocative communication. Every slow stroke, every luscious sweep of his tongue against hers designed to gain her trust. A soothing rhythm, more waltz than battlefront.

Rashid sensed what burned behind the passion and the taking. Anger. She was deeply hurt. Deeply angry. Her surrender would not come easy. He could feel it still. The resistance. Her stand-alone that spoke more of frightened child than cool woman. There was nothing cool about this woman—nothing he couldn't salve with dedicated attention to her every desire.

Never had he been so determined to temper the appetites that raged in his system. This was about the journey. The journey from stranger to lover; from fear to intimacy. It was a journey he sensed she hadn't travelled before. Not fully. He wanted to take her there. To ease her over that sensual threshold. He wanted her trust. He wanted her surrender.

He took their kiss from easy to evocative.

When Rashid lifted his mouth from hers, Jemma nearly floated from the silken magic he'd spun.

"I want to pleasure you."

His words were distant, as if she'd ventured too far away.

"Oh, you've pleasured me, Your Highness." She struggled to focus, to recapture her wayward senses.

His wicked mouth journeyed further, his hands on a leisurely traverse. A soft keening sound came from her lips as he cupped her breasts. Hell. She was on a slow road to hell... joyously frustrated, blissfully provoked... and crazy impatient. She reached for him, but his hands captured hers and held them prisoner. His tongue lavished her neck, his hot breath like sin itself. She wanted to touch, to rush, to get on with finding that peak they both sought—that *she* sought—but instead found herself languidly wanting. His mouth traced a burning path to her yearning breasts—and on to the flat plane of her belly.

"That's some time management system you've got going there, Your Highness. You need to move this along."

"There's a time for rushing, Jemma, but this isn't it..." His words cut off as he ventured lower, his fiery breath skimming a place that had her body pitching, her head pressing into the pillow, and her teeth digging into her lips. For a man who didn't want to rush, he moved with stealthy speed past the main event and down to her inner thighs. His hands released hers and instead worshipped the length of her leg, the flesh of her thighs, her calves, her feet, her toes. Oh, stop. Now. She went to move, but he stayed her with one dark scowl through lashes, rich and thick. Oh, please. She wanted to participate, to direct, but Mr. Holier-than-thou would have none of it. Bossy. Damn superior. Damn masterful with that mouth of his. Those hands.

Call her crazy, but she lost the will to fight. Maybe it was all the pampering she'd received. Her feet had been tended until her strength went to custard and now her whole body was on the way to Custardville. Rashid caressed the arch of her foot, his touch scorching and hungry. Pleasure. Unadulterated pleasure. On that score, she'd been right and then some. He was the kind of man who paid attention. When he rolled her onto her stomach and began the return journey, she thought she'd die. Racked with longing, her body wept with need. When his heavy length brushed against her, she cried out. His hands—large, capable and strong—sculpted her body, turning her bones to liquid.

When he finally flipped her body back to his, she met him mouth to mouth, the smallest of distances between them. With his body weight half on her and half off, she could finally touch. Her hands glided over his muscles, golden and polished in the flickering candlelight. Hard. Tense. Restraint was there, tight and controlled.

It seemed tarrying had cost him as much as it had cost her.

Senses storming, she melded her lips to his and communicated in no uncertain terms just how ready she was to retaliate. Bring it on. She was an equal adversary. It was a knowledge that took her cocky bravado and gave it substance. Confidence. Certainty. He wanted her. He was a man of his word. A man of honour.

"You're beautiful, my Habibti," he murmured, his words

gilded with a barely-there accent, his eyes dark and adoring.

His Beloved.

With him, for him, she was a woman undone. She wanted him more than any other. Her heart thudded with the truth of it. She felt beautiful, desired, cherished. Which was… crazy. Hell, she needed to toughen up. He'd knocked her off-centre, messed with her equilibrium.

Her turn to taste. Every rise, every fall, every rounded muscle was a delicious treat. Every groan was a victory won. If he thought she'd linger where he most wanted her to linger, he was wrong. She had every intention of bringing him to the boil, to a place where they could forget this erotic game he'd started and finish it.

Trouble was, she liked his game.

Loved it. There was something to be said for a slow disintegration. Anticipation was a delicious torture. Every lathe of her tongue against him brought pain-filled groans to his lips and she delighted in every one. She played him as she would a delicate instrument—thoroughly—until he growled *no more* and spun her over. He sank his heated mouth onto her breast, and she cried out with every suckle, pull and rasp of his tongue. With every possessive touch against her body.

Her hand sought the small of his back, that dip, that delicious place where every caress snatched his breath, stole his attention and unleashed his hunger. More urgent. More carnal. Every fiery stroke of his tongue drove her mindless with impatience. Her hands roamed the hard curve of his buttocks and her legs wrapped around him.

Leveraging them onto their sides, she sought the velvet steel of him, a mighty handful that sent a thrill through her senses and brought a sharp stop to his breath.

"Very impressive, Your Highness."

Strangled sound. No words. She had him where she wanted him. Powerless. Biddable. She lowered her lips to the hard plane of his torso. Divine. Her mouth was reverent as it ventured lower, her breath brushing the weeping head of him, her hand encircling his entire length before she lowered her mouth and tasted him with provocative delight.

Rashid fought the demons that roared in his ears, the tempestuous fury she unleashed with the hot cavern of her mouth. Her tongue adored him with slow, drugging strokes and curled around him like the proverbial serpent. Her scent was sweet, alluring, intoxicating. Oh, what this woman did to him. She enslaved, mastered, controlled him with predatory ease.

He'd fallen. Hard. For her bewitchment. *Fight.* The silken caress of her hair against his skin, the confident movement of her mouth against him left him weak. More kitten than jungle cat. It had to stop. He pulled away. Released her hold on him. Bereaved the moist heat, the heavenly promise. Breathed deep. Breathed hard. Breathed.

Her mouth landed back on his, demanding, impatient, urgent. She stole the very breath he'd fought so hard to reclaim.

"I want you… inside me. Now."

He devoured her mouth with no apology. No civility. Primal, primitive appetites raged between them, their bodies melded together, hers pressing against him, taunting, tempting, drenched with invitation. He'd be damned if he'd give in now. No. He had a slow hand in mind. A slow taking. A slow ascent. He was no slave to passion. Passion could be tempered, harnessed, enhanced. Mastered. Just like the woman who writhed in his arms.

So easy to sink into that hot heaven.

So easy to give in to the drugging pull.

So easy to claim what was his.

"I want... I want to take you on a journey. Trust me. I know what I'm doing."

"I doubt that, Your Highness."

Snappy. He wanted his name on her lips. There'd be no relief until she cried for Raz. Until that cocky Your Highness was obliterated.

Ragged with desire, he took his time to taste, journeying down to the riches that waited. His mouth sank deep into her lush, simmering flesh and her cry splintered. Every whimper was addictive. Every purr, every muted sob was a cherished reward. Her scent was wickedly good. Her taste, intoxicating. This was heaven. Pure, unadulterated pleasure. He circled the velvet heat of her entrance with his tongue and gently ventured into the drenched depths, drawing a long moan from her lips, a sigh, a grinding lift of her hips. With tongue and hand, he delivered a sensual ultimatum.

Damn the man to hell. He had the devil's tongue and the devil's will.

Jemma teetered on a sensual precipice. Just as her body prepared for flight, he withdrew and left her furiously frustrated. His breath fanned her face. His weight lowered against her, his body ramrod hard. She fought the desperation, the sensual fog, the furious force of her heartbeat. Pushed through the stupor and glared at his smug satisfaction. He stroked her face, her cheek, sought God-knew what in the depths of her eyes.

"Your Highness. Finish this or sacrifice me now."

His hands pleasured her breasts and left her reeling, ensnared in the dark depths of his gaze. His touch was a royal pain. *He* was a royal pain. He rolled her onto him, his turgid thickness a royal temptation. All she had to do was slide back, take him inside and soothe the need, the hunger, the longing.

He took her face in his palms, brought her mouth back to his and tasted with reverent quiet. Damn him. Why did he have to go and make it feel like more than it was? She didn't want this to feel meaningful. She didn't want the special. The magic. She didn't want to feel… like this. This was much more than a physical ache. She ached to the core. To her heart. To the depths of her being.

His thumbs wiped her cheeks.

She was crying? "Damn you, Raz." The words were wrung from lips that clung to his. Damn him. She fought the emotion in his kiss, tried to take it back to the physical. Fought the connection. Fought the slow. Took his thick, impressive length into her slick wet centre. She wasn't sure if she slid back or he lifted up. Her head was lost in his taste, in his tongue, in the allure of his mouth. In the feel of him inside her body. She welcomed his invasion, his possession. He claimed her fully. Swept away in a sensual storm, she moved against him. His mouth lavished her breasts and she flew high, sensation rocketing through her like a blast.

Never had she been taken so completely. So blessedly.

This was a communion at so many levels. One she could do nothing to stop. It razed her like fire, it took her to places she'd never been before. From tempest to roar. From roar to scream. From scream to storm. She shattered, splintered, soared. He was with her, inside her, his body tight, his climax as gravity-defying as hers. And when they were spent, when the crazy kathump of her heart slowed and he cradled her against him, the tears came. What the hell had they done? Her tears were from pain as much as from ecstasy. He'd taken her to paradise. One as beautiful as it was blissful. She felt safe. She felt cherished. She felt loved.

He was the Prince of Zahidah. The father of her child. Guilt snapped at her and she snapped right back. So, it wasn't a match made in heaven and couldn't go any further than this. It wasn't like it was her first one-night stand. No, it was her second… with the same man, so theoretically, it wasn't a one-night stand, it was a two-night stand. When her breath was no longer a fragment of glass in her throat, she set about making it less.

"Not bad, Your Highness." Her words were slurred.

"Not bad?" he grumbled.

"Not bad beats not good."

"I'll give you not bad…" With a guttural growl, he took her mouth with his. Hers was equal in every way. Okay. So they had some mighty big pheromones to deal with. Giant pheromones. Demanding pheromones.

Pheromones she could handle.

Princes not so much.

His hands adored her body and his mouth adored, well, her, and she couldn't muster any resistance. She couldn't remember why she couldn't just go where he led. She was biddable. Pliable. Compliant. Oh, yes. Already there was the lick of flames, the spark of more.

The man was a magician.

Spellbound, she followed where he led. Down paths she'd taken only with him. With Rashid beside her, his hands holding hers, palms pressed together, bodies in synch, she felt… something deep and fulfilling. When they collapsed beside each other, her body weak from his thorough retaking, she couldn't speak. No witty come backs. Nothing to push him away.

"Jemma?"

"Hmmmm?"

"Time to rest."

"Hmmm." If her body was any more relaxed, she'd pour off the bed. She curled up against him and let him harbour her, finding what she'd always hoped to find, but never trusted she would. Peace. With him. For now.

Chapter Ten

"Where's Rashid?" Jemma opened one eye to find the bed empty and the two girls from the day before waiting for her.

"He left to meet with the Daiji Imam."

"He didn't mention it."

"He had other things on his mind."

"Yes." Jemma swallowed against the moment of awkwardness, the blade of disappointment in her throat. She'd hoped to see him, but of course, he had responsibilities, duties. His life wasn't his own. Not truly. Which gave her pause. Aminah's life wasn't her own either. She really hadn't appreciated that before. Her eyes widened when she saw the time. Mid-morning? She had things to do today. Like find Aminah. She leapt out of bed, relieved the women had come for her.

"Are we too late to go to the waterhole?"

"No, but we were about to wake you. Soon it will be too hot."

The girls helped her with her preparations for the day. After a modest breakfast of fire-baked bread and dried fruits, she gulped from an earthenware bowl of water.

"Let's go." Her Zahidan was slower than theirs but good enough to communicate.

The heat of the sun was already fiery. People sat in the shade, the older men smoking from ancient pipes. The sand was hot beneath her sandals and the air was thick. She moved through it slowly as if through sticky syrup.

The waterhole was a popular place and the sound of voices rang loud. Here, the women jostled with each other and chatted as they stood in thigh deep water washing clothes and dishes. Children splashed in the shallows and there was a carnival atmosphere. Water. The reason for the age-old wars. In New York, it had seemed farfetched, but here, in the perpetual oven that was the desert, she could see why people would kill for the blessed relief of it. She sighed as the cool liquid spilled over her feet and she waded out into the depths. She allowed the voices to wash over her, but filtered the words, trying to make sense of them.

With her camera in hand, she captured the laughter of the children and the simple pleasure of the women. There was no talk of the princess.

Jemma drew them into conversation. She showed the screenshots of the children to the mothers and promised to send photos and ventured closer to the questions she needed to ask. Had they heard of the missing princess?

Would Husam risk death to steal Aminah? Would he kidnap her to avoid handing over the land his forefathers had fought for and won?

Perhaps death was not a threat to him. To some men, it was an honour. To others an escape from the pain of love or grief. She knew the dangers of that, the allure of death to men of a certain frame of mind. She had pulled her father back from that edge often enough.

The thought of news of Aminah made her insides dance like moths against lantern glass... Aminah's safety was all that mattered. Later, she would speak with Rashid. He loved his sister, but he wanted what was best for Zahidah. She needed to tell him about the book. Their goal had been leverage for Aminah's freedom rather than publication, but time was against them.

One of the girls pointed out Layla. She was slim and beautiful. She leaned over the water, a small distance from the rest, intent on her task. Husam's attendant. Thanking her guides, Jemma waded over. She pondered how best to broach the subject as she directed her lens towards the splashing play of the children, the bright colours of the women washing the clothes.

"Hello. I'm Jemma." She indicated to the thick lens on her camera. "Can I take your picture?"

The woman smiled and nodded.

"Thank you." Picture taken she showed it to her. It was the best one yet. "I understand you're Husam's personal attendant?"

"One of them."

"Have you heard of Princess Aminah?"

The woman reacted as if Jemma had splashed her with cold water, but she coolly recovered. "Why do you ask?"

"I would like to speak with Husam."

"He will not speak with you. I have heard the talk. You are Prince Rashid's lover."

"Yes." His lover. The words prickled over her skin like a cool breeze. "But I wish to speak with him regarding Princess Aminah's disappearance. Privately."

"Why?" The woman's black eyes shone with intelligence. She was no fool and talking about Husam behind his back was not wise from her perspective. Layla should have thought of that before boasting to her friends.

"I understand you can't betray Husam. That's admirable. Smart."

The woman nodded.

"I need to find Princess Aminah. I think Husam may know where she is."

The woman shook her head. "I don't think so. Why do you say these things?"

Jemma considered her options. "Can you pass a message on to Husam?"

"That depends on what it is."

Sheesh. "Sheikh Kamil will not want to marry Aminah when he learns of it." That was part of their plan. Aminah's illegitimacy was the perfect *un*hook. Sheikh Kamil would lose interest in Aminah faster than ice would melt in the desert. "There's nothing to be gained from hiding Aminah from Sheikh Kamil."

"Why would he do that in the first place?"

"To protect the land won by his grandfather. Will you tell him?" She couldn't keep the anxiety from her voice.

"I will tell him, but I'm sure he knows nothing of the princess's whereabouts."

The woman would make a brilliant poker player. Her expression was soft and celestial. "Thank you. I appreciate that. If it turns out he has information that could help me find her, could you please let me know? I'm very worried about her."

"If Husam knows anything, which I doubt. Yes."

"Thank you."

The woman turned her attention back to the clothes she was washing.

"Would you like some help?"

"Sure."

The two women fell into a companionable silence, their hands busy at the task. Jemma's mind skittered away. Would Husam send her a message? Did he have any information that would help her find Aminah?

Rashid stormed into the tented bedroom. The talks were not progressing. He needed to find Aminah. He needed the damn marriage to go ahead and soon before war broke out and innocent people died. Where was Kamil? The sheikh needed to be here to temper the fiasco that was brewing. He'd made a grave error of judgment bringing Jemma into a situation that was this unstable. His questions to the Imam had resulted in very little information regarding his sister. If the Imam knew of her whereabouts, he'd denied it vehemently. There was nothing to suggest the Daijis were involved in Aminah's disappearance and now he was faced with the growing fear that he'd put Jemma's life in danger. The Daijis did indeed have something to gain from the wedding not going ahead. She'd been right about that. Could they have had a role in his sister's disappearance? He couldn't rule it out.

If there was a way to search the Daiji camp, his security people would find it. If Aminah was there, mayhem would result. He'd had enough of their impertinence. Where was Jemma? He paced the carpeted area of their quarters, his scowl deepening by the moment. Damn her. What he wanted was to lose himself in her body—fast and furious—the way she'd wanted it. His patience had worn thin. All day he'd suffered from the relentless aftermath of a night like none he'd known before. Her sweet scent, like gardenia or frangipani, filled his head. What he wanted, what he wanted... was to do it all over

146

again. What he needed was Jemma. Her snappy mouth. Her serpent tongue. Her reverent touch. Today he'd walked the planet like a god. Like a king. Never had he revelled more in his role than he had today.

But now? The truth was clear to him. He'd never wanted a woman more. Not just her body. *Her.* He wanted to talk with her. To share his fears. To seek her opinion. To burden her with affairs she had no business being a part of. She was here because he'd given her no choice. With him—*to scratch an itch.* The thought deepened his scowl. Women. Could any of them be trusted? Look at his mother. Look at Fadila. Look at Jemma and her poor husband.

Jemma had planned to help Aminah disappear. Another week and the result would have been the same. A different motive. A different person responsible. Same end-result. Women were deceitful. Period. Beautiful on the outside, rotten to the core.

Where the hell was she?

He paced from one end of the room to the other. Outside, the sun was scorching. Rest was the preferred activity. Too hot to talk, to walk, to think. Where the hell was she? It wasn't safe outside. It wasn't safe inside with the demons that raged in his head. In his body. Where was Aminah? The questions were driving him to the brink of crazy. And where was Jemma? Truly? There was nowhere to disappear to. Just endless sand. They were days from another source of water. And therein lay the problem.

The Daijis could hold the Zahidans to ransom. The spring was located on the Daija side of the boundary. It fed the pool his people relied on. A stretch of water that crossed the boundary between the two countries. Cooperation was essential for his people's wellbeing but being subservient to the Daijis for water was intolerable. Water. More precious than oil, although God knew the riches underneath that land would keep his people prosperous for generations to come. How was he to keep his promise to his grandfather? The marriage couldn't go ahead. Not with honour. Not if his sister wasn't who the sheikh believed her to be. An illegitimate princess would hardly have the same appeal. Of course, once they were married and the deal was done regarding the transfer of land title, would it matter?

To him, yes. Honour was important. More important than water? Than his people's well-being? Sheikh Kamil would have to be told of Aminah's disappearance and when the results of Rashid's own tests were through, her parentage. Rashid's father would disagree, but Rashid would demand it. His father was in his eighties. He was tired and less and less able to manage the demands of directing their country into the future. It was the only option. Perhaps with her marriage off the agenda, Aminah would feel safe to come home. If she had a choice.

"Are you carrying *all* the worries of the world there, Your Highness?"

The witch herself. "It's a prince's duty. Where have you been?"

"Washing clothes. It's a woman's duty."

Facetious.

"No, a woman's duty is to satisfy her man." He drew her towards him, his mouth the merest distance from hers.

"Is that what I am? Your woman?" Fiery back-at-you flared in her eyes. Eyes that stole the breath from his lungs. Translucent turquoise. More beautiful than a coral sea. Her hands skated down his back and lingered in a place that pressed him closer to her soft, ripe centre.

"Your eyes are stunning." Spellbound, he studied their pristine depths. They fascinated him. Like the sun searing the ocean all the way to the seabed. They brought him to his knees, a hair's breadth from a blithering idiot. They sapped his brain of thought and seized his synapses. She was his focus. Entirely. Everything else ceased to exist.

Her pleasure. *Her* readiness. *Her* slick, scalding heat.

He pulled her against him, and she gasped, her breath as jagged as glass. She felt it, too, then. That yearning need. That drugging desire. Her mouth lured him to sup. To taste. To take. He walked her backwards, tight in his embrace, until the back of her knees hit the bed.

"Distracted, Your Highness?"

"I'm one hundred percent focused. *On you.*" He tipped her back onto the mattress and followed her mouth with his. His skin was electric. His body fractious. "And I'm feeling a need to rush."

"Thou of the slow hand?"

Her hand traced that part of him that was beyond ready for her. Vixen. She drove him to the brink of crazy with a single touch. He closed the miniscule distance between their lips and gorged on the delights that awaited him. Her kiss was an aphrodisiac. He fought her clothes and his own and freed himself in a rush before sinking into her warm welcoming heat. All of the wound-up-harried inside of him erupted in a joining that was as desperate as it was tender, voracious as it was considerate. No master and mistress here. Jemma was with him, beside him, urging him on, all the way. The connection he found with Jemma was magical. She earthed him, settled him, calmed him even as his release detonated and her body clutched and held and pulsed around his. Even as he soared to heights of sensation that he'd experienced with no one, but her.

When his heartbeat ratcheted back from frenetic to furious to fast, he drew her close and their mouths fused with something he couldn't yet verbalise. With Jemma, he found solace. With Jemma, he escaped the chains that bound him, all thoughts of duty and princely responsibility blasted from his head. She released him from Zahidah, from the role he revered and hated. She was a place of sanctity. Of blessed renewal. Rejuvenation. Far from depleted, he felt refreshed. With Jemma in his arms, he slept. Fully. Deeply. Freely. For the first time in years.

Jemma woke to a frantic whisper in her ear, a gentle yank on her sleeve. What was it? Where was Rashid?

"Miss Jemma, wake up."

"What is it?"

Layla looked furtively behind her. "Husam will speak with you. Come."

Jemma reached for her clothing and dressed in haste, the rush of adrenaline making her clumsy.

"Why are we whispering?"

"Because you mustn't draw attention and you need to hurry. Rashid gave orders you were not to be disturbed, but someone may come. Arrange the cushions under the sheet."

"How do you know?"

"I waited in the shadows until it was clear. Let's go. Quickly. Before they stop us. Husam would be in grave danger if anyone knew he was to meet with Rashid's mistress."

"Of course." Layla was heavily veiled. Her sideways glances

and stealthy steps spoke of anxious vigilance. Perhaps Husam knew of Aminah's whereabouts. The thought was a golden carrot that pushed Jemma to ignore caution and follow Layla. She knew of the tensions between the Daijis and the Zahidans. If they had Aminah, they could hardly hand her back without the risk of war.

There had to be a solution. She would work it out.

With a veil covering her head and her face, she was sheltered both from recognition and the harsh heat of the sun. Its vicious burn was still there despite the late hour of the afternoon and the shadows that had lengthened across the sand. The smell of cooking was rich and spicy on the air, and Jemma's stomach growled. They circled the tented community and headed across an open stretch towards the waterhole, their behaviour casual, as if they were off to bathe.

But they didn't venture close to the pool of water where the children frolicked.

There was no lessening of Layla's tension as they neared the Daiji camp. Her movements were jerky, her voice quiet. Her grip on Jemma's arm was like a bony clamp. There was no need for pressure. If she led Jemma to Aminah, Jemma would willingly follow her anywhere.

Layla stopped at a richly furnished tent and they discarded their sandals before entering. Inside it was blissfully cool and dark. It took Jemma's eyes a moment to adjust, her feet sending messages of heaven to her brain as she stepped onto beautiful, textured rugs.

"Husam?"

Layla pushed through a heavy curtain that partitioned the space and Jemma found herself in the presence of a young man who oozed self-importance. He sat cross-legged on huge cushions, a low table before him. Light came from a lamp, but it was muted and flickery. Dark shadows rested on his face, but Jemma could see it was finely hewn, almost beautiful. His nose was straight, his skin tanned. He had a long beard that shadowed his jaw with an almost holy look.

"Sit," Layla urged, her voice husky. Gone was the strangled whisper. Jemma was surprised by what she saw on the young woman's face. A warmth of feeling that spoke of confidence and intimacy. Secrets shared.

The man gestured to the cushion across from him and dismissed Layla with a nod. The woman retreated, her head bowed, her body bent like a willow.

Jemma's mind raced as she sat.

The fellow turned his gaze towards Jemma and for the shortest moment she pondered his black, generously lashed eyes. They were eyes she would know anywhere. She leapt from her seat and bounded onto the poor chap, knocking him from his cushions.

"Aminah?" she yelped. "You're okay? You're alive."

"Shhh," she grumbled. "Are you trying to expose me? Do you want me married off to an elderly man who'll rut like a beast?"

"I'm so relieved to see you." Jemma frisked the feminine body inside the manly clothes for injury. "You're truly okay? You're not hurt? I've been so worried."

"It's a long story." The dark eyes, liquid with emotion held hers. "I'm sorry, Jemma. I know you must have been worried. I was taken by the Daiji's but... Rashid can never know that. He would demand revenge. War would break out. I'm okay. I'm more than okay."

With eyes adjusted to the muted light, Jemma could see the strain around the corners of Aminah's eyes, the darker skin beneath. "If you were kidnapped, how did you get permission for me to come?"

"So many questions."

Jemma turned and saw a handsome young man, features chiselled, his square jaw dark with stubbled growth. His robes were white, setting off his dark tan but nothing could hide the granite-like physique beneath or the flash of his smile. "Are you Husam?"

"Yes," he said with a warm glance in Aminah's direction.

What was going on? She saw the coy drop in Aminah's gaze and realised she liked him. Loved him? Had she fallen for him? It was not impossible, she realised.

"We must tell Rashid it was my doing," Aminah said, her voice soft and melodic, the false beard on her chin moving with every word.

"Aminah." Husam's voice was sharp and his expression was filled with love for her.

"If we say it was my idea," she persisted, "then Husam is innocent. It makes sense that he would want to stop the marriage as much as I did." Her voice was shaky. "So, I asked him for help." Aminah lifted her head, her beautiful eyes settling on Jemma. "We could say Layla helped stage my disappearance. Your innocence has been proven and I will prove Husam's as well. I'm sorry you were worried."

Aminah was safe. Aminah was fine. Aminah was alive. Jemma's body crumpled as a wave of relief washed through her. Thank goodness.

"I don't know whether to thank you or chastise you," she said as she swiped the wetness from her face.

"Thank me." Aminah's eyes glittered and her attention shifted to the young man whose gaze was never far from hers.

"And thank Husam."

"You have feelings for him?" Jemma whispered, her face angling towards Aminah.

"Yes," she said with a soft smile.

The young man lowered himself to sit with the two women, his gaze intense. "If Rashid discovers his sister here, he will want payment in blood. We are on the verge of war as it is. This could tip the scales toward violence before we have a chance to explain."

Husam's words left her frozen. Jemma had meddled in something she didn't understand.

"Rashid will be relieved his sister is safe. He is a man of honour." The truth of it struck her with force. Rashid was a good man. A man of strength. A man who could be trusted to do what was right. A man who would put his people before himself. "He would thank you for taking care of his sister if he believed she came to you of her own volition."

Husam settled himself onto a cushion. "Aminah told me the king is not her father. She told me of your plan."

"Any day now, our book will be published. We need to use it to convince Rashid to change his mind. Sheikh Kamil will not want the marriage to go ahead. Not when he discovers how far Aminah will go to avoid it. But I…"

"What treachery is this? Why are you sharing this with my enemy and not with me?"

Rashid's voice was deep and whip-like. Jemma's heart leapt. She had rehearsed the telling so many times, but never had she envisaged the dark anger she saw etched into his stony expression. Nor had she felt so poorly, like the worst kind of vermin.

"Rashid?"

"Did you think I would leave you unguarded in this danger-ous place? You would be a prize for my enemies indeed. Little did I know how much!"

His fury stormed around her, but she sat eerily still in the middle of it. He didn't recognise Aminah. Her mind spun with the implications. Aminah was safe. Husam was not. If she could just distract him. "How much did you hear?"

"Enough to know the extent of your treachery. You would expose my family secrets in a book and bring shame to Zahidah? Danger to my mother? And you conspire with my enemy?" His robes billowed as he paced, his sandaled feet, dusty from his hasty passage. "Betrayal comes with a double X gene."

He'd followed her? He'd sought to protect her? Jemma's strength splintered and something deep inside her hollowed and caved and collapsed. Had anyone truly cared for her safety before? Ever? She physically crumpled, the acid from her stomach rising and burning like poison in her throat.

"You lay with me, the truth masked behind those eyes, as clear as glass. You are as tainted as any of your kind." His eyes had daggers in their indignant depths.

Loathsome emotions unfurled inside her: guilt, shame, and disappointment. Where was the anger that kept her strong? The outrage she harnessed to push the feelings back? Snappy, snarky, sassy dissipated into thin air. She shivered as if ice had lodged beneath her skin.

"Nothing to say, Jemma? No smart comeback? No 'this is *your* fault'?"

"Prince Rashid." Husam's voice was rough with emotion and fatigue as he rose to his feet. "The marriage agreement was wrong from the outset. The land was paid for with my people's blood. It belongs to us. It's not for barter."

"And yet your blood is that of a coward, Husam. Kamil will no doubt be interested to discover how far the Daiji people will go to undermine his authority."

"The sheikh was wrong to interfere in a dispute that has nothing to do with the ruling family…"

"It has everything to do with the ruling family. Without leadership, there is disorder, chaos, war, bloodshed, and death. Our children need to play and swim and grow in safety. This land belonged to Zahidah for centuries before your grandfather stole it from mine. If you want to bring strength and economic stability to your people, and be competitive on the world stage, you need to stop this discord with Zahidah. The world is bigger than the microcosm within which you strut." He finished his final sentence with a flourish.

"Sheikh Kamil would have discovered the truth," the young man declared with an arrogant lift of his chin. "And questioned your honour. But there is a better solution." He stood, his height not quite that of Rashid's. "If you are willing to listen." He waited a full two minutes before he continued. "*I* will marry Aminah." He raised his chin. "If she will have me. We will rule the land together. Peace will come to our people. A collaborative government will be formed between Daija and Zahidah."

Aminah leapt to her feet.

"Who is this?" Rashid demanded.

"Husam is right. Our marriage would enable you to keep your promise to our grandfather. There must be time to stop the book from being published. Now that you know. It was not Jemma's idea. It was mine. I was desperate to avoid Kamil. The thought of marriage to him was worse than death. I'm sorry, but you wouldn't listen. No one would listen to me. Except Jemma, who put her own life in danger to help me."

"Yet more treachery, Jemma?" Rashid hurled his anger like a flaming arrow. "You knew Aminah was here?"

"No, this is not Jemma's fault. It's mine." Aminah stood beside Husam. "I chose to come here. I asked Husam for his help. He is kind, compassionate and clever. I would be proud to be his wife." Her gaze softened and her hand came to rest in his.

Rashid held his silence for a stony eternity. His face gave nothing away. Jemma's breath stagnated in her lungs, lights flashing in the periphery of her vision. Aminah wanted to marry Husam? Breathe. Breathe, she reminded herself. Soundlessness rang in her ears. Rashid stood still, his spine strong, his muscles tense—slingshot ready to move. It was uncomfortably tense, the air a vibration against her skin.

"My younger sister, it seems," he said at last, his voice regally controlled, "has found a workable solution of her own. I am relieved you are safe, Aminah. For that, Husam, I thank you. You are my friend, my enemy, and now it seems… my brother-to-be. There is much to discuss." Rashid's composure was outstanding. Jemma couldn't have been more proud. He was truly a magnificent man. "Come. We will find the Imam. Sheikh Kamil is due to arrive any moment and needs to be informed. We will leave the women to get reacquainted and then Jemma," he turned his gaze, cool and calculating towards her, "you will tell me what arrangements are necessary to stop the publication of this accursed book."

The men prowled from the room like lions, without a backward glance. Silence fell and Aminah's sobs rent the air. Jemma turned to comfort her.

"Aminah, I'm so proud of you. He needed to know about the book, but I was so afraid to tell him. I was worried if I told him, you'd have nothing to negotiate with. I feared it would be published before we found you and the impact would be catastrophic for Nada and the Zahidan people. Now Rashid will stop its publication and you are free of your obligation to Kamil." Jemma wrapped her arm around the young woman's shuddering form and allowed relief to wash through her like a wave.

Aminah smiled at Jemma through her tears. "I'm so happy. After everything we've been through. Who would have thought?" They held each other for a long, recuperative moment until Aminah's voice broke the quiet. "You lay with him? With Rashid? Do you love him after all? Will you tell him about Sami?"

"No." The word rushed from Jemma's lips. "I can't." She stepped away, crossing her arms as if suddenly chilled. Aminah couldn't be more wrong. Nothing had changed. She couldn't tell Rashid about Sami, nor did she love him. She hungered for him. Yes. But love? No. Besides, Rashid would never forgive her. Not now. She'd seen it in his eyes. She would leave. Go back to her life. Aminah was found. Where joy should have triumphed, shadows lurked. Stifling ones. "I admire and respect him though. He was deeply troubled by your disappearance." That much was true. But how could he ever forgive Jemma for colluding with Aminah to publish her story? "It is best this way. I need to get back to Sami and to my work. Your dreams will come true with Husam and we will see each other often. This is a good solution."

"Your roots are in Zahidah."

"I love and hate Zahidah." She loved and hated Rashid. The

knowledge hit her like a mountain of rock. He'd moved her like no other man. Taken her to places no other man had taken her. He'd reached her. Undaunted by the myriad of barriers she hid behind—the shields that kept her safe. *She* was a coward. It was an uncomfortable realisation. Through Rashid, she'd seen herself as she truly was. Lonely. Afraid. It was a sight that threatened her sense of self. She was strong. She was loyal. But love? She didn't want it. She didn't need it. She'd suffered enough. Love was for those who dreamed. She was a realist. A survivor. A loner.

She didn't need Rashid's good opinion of her.

She didn't need his touch. His kisses. His royal interference in her life.

She didn't need his love. His or any other man's.

She didn't want it. She had Sami. And for Sami, she would walk away.

Chapter Eleven

"I thought you'd be halfway to anywhere but here." Rashid's voice interrupted the quiet of the night. He'd pushed the curtain aside to enter their private domain, only to stop when he saw her.

Jemma struggled up, drawing the sheet with her, fully awake. She'd tried to sleep, but with every sense alert for Rashid's return, the mattress was a bed of nails. The soft, flickering light from a bedside candle illuminated the deep furrows on his brow, the shadows under his eyes. He hadn't shaved and his jaw was dark with stubble. He ran his fingers through his hair, and it stuck up at odd angles, scruffy and delicious. Reaction shot to her centre and there it was. The truth. He moved her in ways that made her want to smooth the worry away; to ease the burden; to take some of the load. She yearned to comfort him. To... love him.

"It was tempting with Sheikh Kamil's helicopter just sitting there, his pilot nowhere to be seen. Easy pickings," Jemma agreed.

"There I was, thinking you'd abscond with a vehicle and foolishly attempt to cross the desert on your own at night. You can pilot a helicopter? But of course, you can. Is there anything you can't do?"

His question was a rhetorical one. Gone was the push-pull connection they'd shared. Resignation? Where was the fight she coveted? The joyous friction that powered their attraction?

"Rashid, about the book…"

"There's nothing you can say right now that will change what is. Aminah is free of her marital obligation. As you cleverly conspired. I admire your process. Single-minded. Never mind the people you hurt or shame in the process. You can tick Aminah off your to-do list. Done. Mission accomplished. Although I don't think you anticipated her feelings for Husam."

"The book was our insurance policy and it was cathartic for her to tell her story. For too long, she felt invisible. Trivial. A commodity to be traded at your discretion. It gave her a voice. It gave her the confidence she needed to take the next step. And no, I didn't anticipate her feelings for Husam."

Rashid lowered himself onto the bed and Jemma gripped the sheet tighter as if to shield herself from his disregard. He was robed, but his lean, muscular torso was etched in her memory. The satiny hardness, the rippling strength. Her mouth was drier than the windswept plains beyond their walls. How could she fix this?

"Kamil has graciously accepted Aminah's marriage to Husam without the need to hear of her illegitimacy."

"I'm relieved to hear that."

"There's no need for you to concern yourself further. No doubt you plan to return to your daughter at the first opportunity. We will begin our return journey to the city tomorrow at first light. Then you are free to go. I'll detain you no further."

He stood and walked back to where the curtain separated the bedroom from the other partitions.

"Your Highness, this is *your* bed."

"I'll rest elsewhere."

His departure was akin to having a vital organ wrenched from her body.

Aminah was free. *She* was free. Her head spun as if her blood had leached to the floor. His disillusionment was like acid in her veins. An acid that burned and cut and devoured her flesh. What was wrong with her? How could the very thing she'd yearned for—escape for Aminah—hurt so much? What had she done? Had she fallen in love with Rashid? The thought was sour even as the words formed.

No.

Lessons from her childhood came flooding back.

The emptiness. The agony of wishing, wishing, wishing for her father's love. It had weakened and possessed her and driven her to want and yearn and ache for something she just couldn't have. Better to stand alone. To stand strong. She didn't want it. She wasn't going to fight for something she didn't want. Thanks, but no thanks. Walk away. Leave his royal highness to be a royal pain in the butt to someone else. She didn't need his judgement. His royal put-downs.

Good.

She would get sorted. Go back to the apartment. Pack up their things and get Sami home to Australia via New York. She needed to visit Nola. She had some explaining to do.

Where was Rashid? Had he gone to another woman's bed? Had his Royal Highness moved on before her side of the bed had even cooled? Good to know where she stood. One woman was as good as any other to him. She curled her knees closer to her chin. She didn't do emotional involvement for a reason. It damn well hurt. She wasn't the masochistic kind. Better to make a clean break and leave him to someone else.

His words echoed in her head. *You're as tainted as the rest of your kind.*

The disappointment in his voice had lacerated deeper than a physical strike.

He'd been hurt.

She'd betrayed him and she could only hope he'd understand later, with time. His mother had conceived a child with another man whilst married to his father. His sister had reneged on her agreement to marry Sheikh Kamil and disappeared into the ether, albeit not her fault, leaving him unable to fulfil his obligations. His fiancée had all but left him at the altar. A pregnant virgin. Was it any surprise he'd reacted the way he had? She'd neglected to mention the book for a reason. It was their secret weapon. Their final strike. She'd needed it to be as potent as possible. So where was the air-punching thrill of victory?

Or had she kept it from him to hold on to that tenuous feeling between them for as long as she could? In the first instance, she'd sought to help Aminah. Now, it was about Rashid and it was too late to go back. She should have told him about the book. But the book was a step too far. The more she'd gotten to know him, the more awful the book had become. Too awful to forgive. She'd helped Aminah find her voice, but the cost had been greater than she could have imagined. Rashid would fix it. That's what he did. The cost was something she'd have to live with. Like her father had done. Pining for a love he couldn't have. She was not her father. She rejected the thought even as she rejected the weakness that flowered deep inside.

She had Sami and she would never do to Sami what her father had done to her.

She couldn't blame Rashid. His reaction was everything

she'd known it would be. The very thing she'd tried to protect herself from. She'd failed miserably.

On the bright side, Aminah was free. Safe from her fear of being married to a man old enough to be her grandfather. They'd taken a stand. A loud one. Aminah had governed her own life *and* met her royal obligations. Jemma couldn't have been more impressed.

Aminah was a princess. The monarchy didn't live by the same rules as the rest of the world. The honour came with responsibility. Duty to the greater good. Leadership demanded sacrifice. Look at Rashid. What would happen to Zahidah if he decided it was all too hard and disappeared into the night? When he married, it would be a careful decision. A woman worthy of Zahidah. Not someone who plotted against his sovereign authority. Not someone who kept the truth of his daughter hidden from him. To love Rashid was just north of crazy, beyond insane and heading full speed towards demented. No. Her feet were solidly connected to the earth, her thoughts rational.

Fantasy and Fancy were dangerous playmates. They spun all kinds of wonderful delusions, desires, and wishes. Like cotton candy, sweet and eye-boggling, but gone the moment it hit the tongue.

Her thoughts hurt, but it was the tears she refused to cry that left her aching.

Rashid settled himself onto a pile of cushions on the floor and let the tension drain from his body. He was tired—exhausted—both physically and mentally. With only an hour or two before sunrise, the negotiations had taken much of the night. He was relieved they had come to a resolution. His anger had burned itself out and he had to admit, his woman was wily.

His woman?

Jemma belonged to no man. That fact had been underscored and highlighted in more ways than he cared to list. She took love where she found it—*on her terms*. When the going got tough, he'd expected her to cut and run. Except she hadn't. He'd expected his bed to be empty. Why had she waited for him? What more did she want? She'd achieved her goal and was more than up to the machinations required to get back to Zahidah alone. She didn't need him. That much was clear.

Her off-the-cuff interference in matters that didn't concern her had been downright... inspired. She'd given Aminah the strength and confidence to find a workable solution for herself. Husam had huffed and puffed like a baby bird desperate to look bigger and fiercer than he was, but when it came down to it, he was the perfect man for Aminah, and their marriage was the perfect solution to centuries of discord. He'd negotiated with Kamil without disclosing the royal family's secrets. A cooperative solution had been found, the most palatable of the options available to him.

Mutual ownership would see his people well cared for into the future. It was one step better than relying on the goodwill of the Daiji people, one step short of his promise to his grandfather. Still, ownership had been reclaimed. No longer could the Daijis divert water to their own country should the whim take them. Zahidah had an equal say in any decisions regarding the diversion of water from one territory to another. Both countries could utilise the water to farming advantage and together, they would honour his commitment to the West. Both countries would prosper for many years to come.

Thanks to Aminah. Thanks to Jemma.

And therein lay the problem.

She'd helped him. She'd betrayed him. She'd supported him, she'd manipulated him. She'd yanked on his chain and petted him at the same time.

She drove him crazy. With lust. With fury. With anger. But no woman had gotten under his skin like she had. Life in his skin wasn't easy. With Jemma, it was better than easy. It was paradise... but without her? The agony was enough to leave him howling at the moon like a man possessed. He wanted her banished to the farthest corner of the earth and he wanted her close. He wanted her burned at the stake—no pyre was high enough—and to lose himself in the heat of her body. The damned woman was the sweetest of poisons. One taste and he was dying—agonisingly—with his need for her.

He couldn't damn well sleep.

He pushed to his feet, jerked the tent flap to the side and strode into the night, the sand soft and cool under his feet. The moon was full and round and high in the sky, lording over a plethora of stars. There was not a breath of wind. Perfect stillness. He nodded to his security staff who blended into the night. He was never truly alone.

What he needed was a solution.

He strode to the edge of the camp and lowered himself to sit. In front of him stretched an endless sea of space. Here, where the earth resembled the heavens. He sat. And waited. Waited for his thoughts to battle and rage and plead and shuffle into some semblance of order. This was about honour. Love versus honour. Honour was the crux of his dilemma.

He watched as the sun eased over the horizon, as the pinks, oranges, and yellows preceded its fiery arrival.

Jemma was far from the future queen of Zahidah. She was a free spirit. Zahidah had taken her mother, her brother. And when he thought about it—though it pained him—her father, too. Her father hadn't been there for her. That much was clear. Unresolved grief? Unrequited love? Who knew? Jemma had been shortchanged.

Jemma's loyalty to Aminah was something to be admired—resented—but admired. And she'd been through hell and back with her daughter's illness. She was a devoted mother. A loyal friend. Her actions—as insidious and disloyal as they appeared—had been driven by her determination to help Aminah. And she had. She'd succeeded where he and his army of security people had failed.

She stood alone.

He pondered the problem as the cool turned to heat, as the colourful pallet in the sky leached away and the harsh sun began its burning arc.

His body fused with the earth. With the savage heart of the desert.

Here, he felt closest to his grandfather, to the lineage that was at the root of every decision he made. But where in the vast solitude was the answer he needed? How could he ask Jemma to stay with him in Zahidah? To sacrifice her freedom? For that was the cost. And then there was Sami. How could his people ever accept a divorced Westerner with a daughter who wasn't his?

This was not a light decision.

His father would fight him. Never had a prince stepped away from the tradition of a chosen bride. Jemma was Zahidan. A technicality since she was Western in every way, right down to the hue of her hair, her pale skin and the aquamarine of her eyes.

How could he ask her to give up the very thing she'd fought so hard to win for Aminah? If he loved her, and he feared he did, he should let her go.

Movement was beyond him but move he must.

Later, as their entourage convoyed through the desert, he sat in silence beside the woman he wanted more than breath itself. For long hours, he said nothing. For what could he say? Every word he chose was an unreasonable demand. He stayed silent and said nothing of his desire, his pain, and his hopes for their future.

She, in turn, made no attempt to converse. Her attention was glued to the long shadow of the vehicle as it lurched and slid in the shifting sand. Her back was straight, the traditional robes softening the otherwise steely strength in her spine.

She would leave him. It was there in her steadfast refusal to look at him.

And he would let her go.

Chapter Twelve

J emma and Sami waited in the long queue that wound through the Zahidan airport customs area, their carry-on luggage at their feet. The air conditioning was a blessed relief after the outside heat. The terminal was state-of-the-art. No sign of Zahidah's draconian social system. No sign of its handsome prince. True to his word, he'd dropped her off at her apartment and granted her freedom. Honourable to the last.

After two days of packing and planning, she'd found not the taxi she'd ordered, but a dark-windowed limousine with the palace's insignia waiting at the curb. Clearly, he had kept close tabs on her every move. Fine. He would know that she was headed back to Australia. For half a moment, she'd allowed herself to hope—damn foolish wishes—that he'd be there, in the back, and would plead with her not to go. He'd ask them to stay. Confess he loved her as much as she had stupidly come to love him. Instead, she'd helped Sami into the empty, cavernous space and hadn't been able to delude herself anymore. Forgiveness she didn't deserve.

The beep of a text took her attention from the slow movement of the throng of people, to the cell phone in her handbag.
Fresh news! We have a new boss—one Prince Rashid bin Ra'ed

Al Shahid—who paid an obscene amount of money for the business. When are you back in New York to commiserate over the withdrawal of your book? Nola xx

Jemma texted a reply. She couldn't muster the excitement she should have felt. Rashid had dealt with the problem and both Nada and Zahidah were safe from scandal.

She placed their two passports onto the counter, along with their boarding passes, her mind far from the man who glanced at her photo. His relaxed pose stiffened, and his eyes dodged from the screen in front of him, to her and back again. He directed them to the left, towards a door at the end of the room whilst the flow of people headed to the right.

"Is there a problem?" Jemma queried, her mind shifting back to the now. It was not until several officials in dark uniforms flanked them that she realised they were being ushered away from the public area.

What now? She didn't have any snark left. Nothing in reserve. She just wanted to sink into her seat on the plane, get lost in a movie and find blessed oblivion.

"Are you Jemma Mason?" asked one of the suits. "Is this Sami?"

"Yes."

"What's your birth date? What was your address in Zahidah?" His tone was severe, and he repeated the information she shared into a small microphone that twisted around from his ear, as if checking the data with someone more distant.

This didn't feel right. Something was wrong. Rashid had promised her the freedom to leave. He was a man of his word. Not for one moment had she considered he might renege. Would this nightmare never end?

"Unfortunately, Miss Mason, we have to detain you both.

170

You won't be taking a flight today. Your passport and that of your daughter have been confiscated on the king's orders."

"The king?" Adrenaline snapped in her veins. "Why?"

"The warrant for your arrest suggests you've committed an indictable offence."

"What kind of indictable offence?"

"Publication of propaganda and slander against the king."

Her mind reeled and her heart pounded.

"You'll be detained in a holding cell until charges are laid."

"I'm a dual citizen and my daughter is an Australian citizen. I want the Australian consulate notified of my detainment." Her breath came in short pants.

"That won't be possible."

"It's a basic human right."

"Miss Mason, at this point, you have no rights. The charges against you are very serious indeed. Your daughter is free to go if you have someone to supervise her."

"That's draconian and no, I don't." Margie had left on an earlier flight to get everything ready for their arrival.

"Yes, Ma'am." The official ushered them into a small room with a desk, three chairs, and no windows. The door was locked behind them and Jemma paced the short distance from one wall to the other, over and over.

"Mummy, I don't like it here. Why do we have to wait? I'm hungry."

"Yes, darling, I know. Let's find you a snack and your colouring book. Let's do a picture together while we wait." Jemma forced herself to act like there was nothing to worry about. But inside, she seethed. How could Rashid have gone back on his word? She'd trusted him. She'd believed him. She'd loved him and he'd thrown her to the wolves. Fear unfurled in her belly. It wasn't over. She wasn't safe. Sami wasn't safe.

Forty days in the desert.

The threat was even more terrifying now that she knew of the searing heat and the cruel terrain where not even plants could grow. The endless kilometres of nothing. It was a death sentence. A slow, agonising, barbaric death. They could claim she'd become lost. A tourist who didn't know any better. But what about Sami? Would they die alongside each other after all they'd been through to fight for her life? The royal family could create whatever story they wished and publish it here and in the west. There'd be no repercussions. No one to seek the truth. Here, the word of the sovereign was law. Here, women were at the mercy of men. She knew the truth about Aminah. Did the king plan to silence her? Could she blame him?

Her teeth dug into her lip until the coppery taste of blood distracted her from her thoughts. Snatching up a tissue she pressed it against the flow until it stopped.

Minutes dragged into many more and Sami got tired of drawing. Jemma pulled out her disk player and set up a movie for her to watch. The sound of the door opening was slow to register, but the brush of fabric and the aura of authority was hard to miss.

"So," came a regal voice. "You are Jemma."

The man in front of her was an older version of Rashid. All alpha male, hard planes, and black scowl.

"Yes, and this is my daughter, Sami." Sami barely glanced up, so entranced was she in the story of Cinderella.

If he thought she'd cower, he was wrong. She lifted her torso, found strength in her spine, hardened her gaze. Defiance was like steel in her bones.

"You have been busy," he said with little preamble.

The man lowered himself to sit in front of her, his white robes accentuating the dark tan of his skin. The growth on his face was peppered with white, his skin creased with age. His gaze not only raked the surface of her face but seemed to gouge right through. She refused to flinch. Refused to lower her eyes from his. Black versus aquamarine. Bring it on.

Temper steamed from the long wait. "Why have you detained me? How can you expect my daughter to sit in this room for so long?"

"Your book left me in an awkward position." His gaze was thoughtful.

"None of it is propaganda and you know it. Scandalous maybe, but factual nevertheless and written on Aminah's behalf with her permission." Jemma took a harried breath. "And withdrawn from publication after the publisher was purchased by your son for what was no doubt an exorbitant price."

His scowl deepened. "My wife tells me your actions—as unforgivable as they seem—were grounded in love for Aminah."

"Secrets fester and Aminah was being hurt." Her tone told him loud and clear she would not be bullied by him. "Not to mention being sold off to a man old enough to be her grandfather. She was desperate to feel heard. Desperate to escape. The book was an important part of her healing and important to negotiate her freedom."

"You wrote it for Aminah."

"Yes."

"It had nothing to do with your journalistic hunger for sensationalism? Of wanting another *New York Times* Bestseller at my expense?"

"A happy by-product, but it was unlikely to ever be published."

"And what of my son's enrapt fascination with Miss Jemma Mason? Or is it Mrs or Ms? What do they call divorced women these days? What's your goal there? A royal wedding?"

Jemma leapt to her feet so abruptly her chair crashed onto the linoleum floor and Sami called out in surprise. With both hands pushed forward to stabilise herself, she glared at him. Smug satisfaction twisted his mouth into the semblance of a smile. He was good. He knew just which buttons to press to maximise the hurt.

"What I want is to leave Zahidah and get back to *civilisation*." She twisted the last word, wringing it for every last drop of its essence.

"So, you say. Is that what you're plotting? To drive Rashid to defect from his responsibilities?"

"Never. Rashid is a man of honour. Nothing and no one could come before his commitment to Zahidah. If you knew your son at all, you'd know that wasn't possible."

"Before he met you, I would have agreed."

Jemma's heart leapt. What was he saying? Did Rashid have feelings for her after all? He'd said nothing. Nothing for long hours. Nothing for the two days she'd needed to pack up and leave. He'd had her royally escorted to the airport but still, there'd been no word from him. "Your son has no intentions towards me." She disguised the pain she couldn't hide by bending over and righting her chair. She lowered herself into it.

"My concern is with *your* intentions towards him."

"I have none. My intention is to leave." Damn, where the hell had the tears come from. She'd ached with the need to cry for two days. Now? Now was not the time. She projected ferocity into her facial expression and harnessed her strength.

"We need to leave. With your permission, Your Highness." She couldn't stop the facetious jab.

"That's not going to work."

"Why would you want to keep me here?" Damn stupid female weakness. *Tears Jemma?* What possessed her? Whatever it was, its timing sucked. "Besides, it can't be legal. I want to speak with the Australian consulate."

"I'm told you're Zahidan," he continued, his tone authoritarian, his accent heavy.

"I have dual citizenship. My daughter is an Australian citizen." Sob. Did Rashid know his father was making her life impossible?

"Do you care at all for this country of your birth?"

"No. Yes. Where is Rashid? Does he know of my detainment?"

"No," he replied, without a care.

"With all due respect, Your Highness. You're a bully." She lifted her chin and lengthened her spine as if a puny bit of extra height could make any difference to her dire circumstances. Rashid didn't know. There was something in that. He'd kept his word. The thought was foolishly golden. He'd think she and Sami were happily on their way back to Australia. Aminah would think they were busy getting resettled. In reality, they'd be locked away in an ancient dungeon or, worse, frying in the Zahidan sun and no one would know of their plight until it was too late.

"You're not in a strong position."

She narrowed her eyes into sharp lasers and rose from her seat. "I'm not afraid of you."

"Plucky…" With obvious difficulty, he stood. "…but foolish."

"Where are you going?"

"Unlike you, I'm free to leave."

"What are *your* intentions? You can't hold us endlessly in this room. It's not civil, it's not legal and it's not nice."

"I don't negotiate with people I don't trust."

"I am loyal, trustworthy and true to my word. Each and every adult is entitled to their own opinion, their own choices, their own decisions. You have no right to seek revenge. *I* don't deserve your wrath. Nor does Aminah, nor does your wife. Women in this country are manipulated into marrying men old enough to be their father or in Aminah's case, their grandfather. Your wife was as much a victim of circumstance as you were yourself. Her adultery was rooted in persecution. Your anger is poorly placed if you lay responsibility at *my* feet. The problem is systemic. In my humble opinion, *Your Highness*, your anger should be harnessed for positive change. Zahidah needs to keep up with the rest of the world."

Her cocky bravado deflated, and she sank back into her seat, wrapping her arm around Sami and kissing her on the head. There was little point. She just wanted out of this God forsaken country before it sucked all the life from her veins.

But the desert was a part of her.

It was a truth she hadn't appreciated until that moment. Her flesh was of this dirt, this sand, this country. Her heart was as savage, as raw, as indestructible as the ancient land beneath her feet. She was Zahidan. She belonged here. She felt it. She'd come for Sami and found herself. Unloved, not unlovable. Abandoned, not alone. Independent, not an island unto herself. Rashid had taught her that much. It was a lesson she wouldn't forget. It was a lesson of hope. A bridge of sorts. She too would use her anger for positive change.

"Rashid is of the same opinion. Zahidah needs to change."

The old man moved awkwardly towards the door, and turned, his eyes contemplative as they assessed her face.

She belonged here. In Zahidah. It was a quiet realisation. She was a part of this country of her birth and it was a part of her.

Her attention jolted back to the room when she heard the quiet hiss of the door being opened and closed. It was a simple truth. A part of herself she hadn't recognised. A part of herself she now held dear. A part of Sami she needed to acknowledge and respect.

Her fight had been for Aminah, but it had also been for herself and Sami and the women of Zahidah. For a country that could be better. A country that was her home.

How much longer?

Had they been forgotten?

Jemma strode to the door and tested the handle. They were locked in. Still. Food had been delivered and they'd been offered a bathroom break, but it didn't change the fact that they were being held without explanation. She banged on the door. Infuriated.

"Mummy, when can we get on the plane?"

She stifled her anger. It had spread the gamut from spark to flame to fury and back to ash. Damn Rashid's father. She didn't deserve this. She didn't deserve any of it. Not her father's careless disregard, not Rashid's cold withdrawal, not his father's anger. None of it. She wrapped her arm around Sami and kissed her forehead.

"I'm not sure, Honey Bear. Are you hungry?" Sami shook her head. Jemma swallowed the sob that clawed at her throat. *Smile, damn it.* "Shall we have another game of Uno while we wait?"

"Another movie."

Jemma adjusted Sami's device and settled Sami on her knee. She took ten deep breaths and savoured the scent of Sami's shampoo. Life came with death. Strength with weakness. Courage with fear. Love with hate. Passion with pain. Silence with internal talk.

What did she want from life?

What did she want for her daughter?

For her to know always—deeply—that she was worthy of love. Deserving of love.

To love. And there it was. Like a light in the dark. To be loved was a blessing, but to give love, to love was the essence of happiness. The thought settled in her chest and made itself at home. Both gift and curse because love demanded so much.

Rashid had let her go without a word to dissuade her. He'd given her what he thought she wanted. Her freedom. Wasn't it what she'd fought so hard to win for Aminah?

Could he ever understand and forgive her for what she'd done?

Could he love her? Or did he truly want her on the first plane out of his life? Could she risk telling him the truth about Sami? He was a man of honour. He had a right to know and there it was… the familiar stirring of guilt like a cancer inside her. How could she deprive him of his daughter? How could she deprive Sami of her father? The ache in Jemma's chest was a vice and she struggled to breathe. Sami was her world. Sami was her everything.

Rashid was a man of honour. He deserved to know how Aminah had saved Sami's life. He deserved to know the truth. She had to find the courage to tell him. Her heart lurched. She couldn't leave until she'd spoken with Rashid. It was a truth that brought tears to her eyes.

"You what?" Rashid stormed across the stone floor towards the wall and back to his father's desk, his heels loud against the hard surface, his hands fisted into grenades. "You have her in custody? Sami, too? How could you?" He almost burst with the effort of holding back the expletives. His mother stood beside his father, her hand on his shoulder.

"That woman will be charged and sentenced as she deserves. Her book is paramount to treason. She will not leave this country. She will pay for her actions."

"That woman uncovered the truth about Aminah's disappearance. Her actions helped resolve the rift between Daija and Zahidah, without the need to sacrifice my sister or our countrymen. Aminah is happy. The water rights issue is resolved. My promise has been honoured. The book was a threat. Never intended to be published. She did it for Aminah, with Aminah's endorsement, and it has been withdrawn from publication before it hit the shelves. No harm done. Thankfully." Every nerve was reactive to his father's barbs.

"Tripe. She did it for herself. She's a writer. A photojournalist. She knew that book would be a bestseller. At my expense. At your expense. At the expense of this country and the credibility of our standing in the Western world."

His father was wrong, and indignation rose in Rashid's throat like an ill-tempered genie released from a bottle.

"I've read it. From my understanding, it's an accurate, factual account. Unless you have evidence to the contrary." Challenge was there in every muscle. Tension arced from sinew to sinew, knotting his neck and shoulders in painful retribution. He

179

kneaded the band of muscle as if he could release the agony of it.

"Why are you defending her?"

Why indeed? It was a question he didn't linger over. He pushed it back at his father like a hot coal passed between them. "There is nothing to be gained from keeping her in Zahidah when her goal is to leave. She can do no further damage. It's not *her* fault there were secrets to be exposed in the first place." He eyed his mother, who stood beside his father, calm and still. "I have a better appreciation of the dangers of forcing women into marriage against their will. It is something we need to consider as a society. This is the twenty-first century. Not the dark ages."

"I got the same forceful message from Jemma. It seems you share a passion about Zahidah's needs for the future. A vision."

"She doesn't care about Zahidah. She has no desire to live here and can't wait to return to her life in Australia…" And Sami's father? Anger snapped and snarled inside him until his face physically ached from the intensity of his scowl. "She is accustomed to liberties Zahidan women are not." The thought of her in the arms of another man was like a dagger to his intestines.

"She was very adamant regarding what Zahidah requires in terms of modernisation. Would someone who cared so little for a country exhibit such passion? She was equally adamant in her defence of your honour. She could not be swayed into thinking you would renege on your word. You are a man of integrity. High praise from someone without feeling for a man or his country. She understands your responsibilities and your honour better than most. I was led to believe she lacked emotion and cared little for anyone but herself. That was not my impression."

"She is untamed, unruly and unlikely to fit the mould required of a royal wife if I correctly understand where you are headed with this conversation. Jemma has lost more than most in her life and was forced to parent her less-than-adequate father. She is strong in a way most women aren't." He stared at his father, overcome with melancholy. "She deserves better than I can offer her. Zahidah is a demanding mistress."

"You're a man pining for a woman." The older man struggled to his feet and took a moment to gain his balance. "I recognise the symptoms. You are useless to your country like this. She has made you weak," he declared.

"She did no such thing. I am strong and fully committed to my country. No woman can change that." Fury blinded him. How dare his father question his commitment to Zahidah. He gave everything to be leader of the damn place. Everything. The burden of it weighed heavily, more stifling than the heat.

"Love makes a man weak," his father persisted. "Arranged marriages work. Leaders cannot afford the distraction of love."

"You're right." Jemma was a distraction. Her scent, the blessed paradise of her body, the challenge of her back-at-you conversation; she was not marriage material. "There is no need to lecture me on the foolhardiness of loving a woman such as Jemma." Emotion dragged at him until he fought for breath. "I know it already."

"You love her?" Nada's voice was gentle. Soft, but strong.

"Yes. No. I don't know." He stumbled over his words and cursed aloud. "The woman scrambles my brain and I can't think straight."

"She tells me we've wasted a valuable resource. That women deserve a say," his father continued.

Rashid couldn't stop the smile that broke through his tumultuous thoughts. That was Jemma, alright. "Jemma's opinion on many subjects is enlightening."

"It is time for a change," Nada urged. "For too long, we have held on to century-old traditions that may have worked in the past but have become outdated and ineffective. It is time to move forward. It is time to consider a more balanced approach to Zahidah's governance. Look at what Aminah has achieved with Jemma's encouragement."

"What are you suggesting?" his father asked.

"I'm suggesting Rashid marry the woman he loves and get on with changing the way things are done."

Rashid moved to assist his father and braced for his opposition.

"A divorced woman with a child?" His father's tone was incredulous.

"An intelligent woman who looks at our son with love in her eyes."

"You said you met her five years ago?" The king studied Rashid, with a look intense enough to blister. "Her four-year-old daughter looks remarkably like you." He was silent for a long moment while Rashid's heart leapt from his chest and raced around the room like an unruly wolf pup. Sami couldn't be his. Could she?

"How could Jemma not tell me if Sami was mine?" The blade deep inside his heart twisted and his thoughts were like shrapnel. Why had she come to Zahidah to find a bone marrow match for Sami? The question should have come to him earlier. He'd assumed it was because her father was Zahidah. More puzzle pieces fell into place. How had Jemma known about Aminah's blood type? Why had she done everything in her power to protect Aminah from a marriage she didn't want? Because Jemma was a good friend? Or because Aminah had saved Sami's life and Jemma owed her?

"She may have decided Zahidah is not the place to raise her daughter. She would not want Sami to suffer like Aminah has. Or Fadila. Or me in the early days of our marriage. She would want to protect her. Jemma is a woman of intelligence and integrity. Of enormous strength. I think she would make an excellent queen," his mother finished

"You do?" Rashid collapsed into the nearest chair. His mind was incredulous. Jemma could be his? *Sami* could be his. Had Jemma left her husband because she was pregnant with another man's child?

"I like her," his mother said. "She has spunk and from what I hear, she's creating quite a stir at the airport. You need to get down there and fix the situation sooner rather than later. And ask about Sami. I may have a granddaughter and I can't wait to meet her." Nada turned to her husband and took his arm.

"Jemma has had plenty of time to stew," his father said with a grin. "She's ready to tear someone's head off and I'd rather it be yours than mine."

"He planned to let her go," his mother muttered. "Our future queen. Without a word of how he feels."

His parents left the room and he stared at the marble floor, his heart swelling. He would just have to tell Jemma how he felt. Sami could be his. How could she not tell him? Because she'd seen the plight of a royal princess firsthand. Because she couldn't trust him not to marry Sami off at the age of nine to some neighbouring sheikh old enough to be her grandfather. Because she wanted to protect Sami from the life of a woman in Zahidah. From royal life and its responsibilities, its burdens.

183

She was a fierce protector. She would do whatever it took to protect her daughter. He saw it clearly now. Women were not treated as equals in Zahidah. Women were not treated with respect. Jemma was a strong, opinionated woman. Strong enough to put Sami's interest before her own. Strong enough to love him and leave him for the good of her child. To keep the truth to herself when it would have been easier to share the burden.

"I didn't raise you to be a coward," Nada said, poking her head back into the room. "What are you waiting for? I want to meet my granddaughter."

"I'm gone." Rashid leapt from his seat and strode past her, taking his mother in a rough hug, anticipation blowing the doom and gloom from his system. He kissed her and held her gaze for a long moment. Her smile was radiant. He hoped she was right. He would tell Jemma how much he loved her and pray she loved him enough to forgive him. He'd been a fool. An arrogant fool. It was unsettling to give another person control over his future. She had the right to a choice and the right to keep the knowledge of his daughter to herself if she believed it was in Sami's best interest. Their child. The thought filled him with hope. He would tell her how much he loved her and pray she trusted him enough to tell him the truth.

He was strong. He could do this.

Chapter Thirteen

Rashid stood before the locked door, his heart in his throat. The small girl he hoped was his daughter was on the other side. The woman he wanted for his bride. He breathed in slowly, braced his spine and settled the hornet's nest of nerves. With shaking hands, he pushed it open. Jemma stood before him, her hands fisted on her hips, her stance wide. There was fire in her eyes and a very short leash on her temper.

"I come in peace," Rashid declared, his hands held high above his head.

"Rashid?" She spun away from him, her heels leaving small indents in the linoleum as she paced this way and that. "You gave your word we were free to leave. Why has your father refused to let us go?"

"I just spoke with him." Rashid closed the door and locked it behind him. He turned and watched the woman he loved, her eyes like turquoise flame. Mesmerising. Gorgeous. Furious.

"What now? Am I to be punished?"

"No, I gave you my word on that," he replied, his tone soothing as if he were handling a panicked horse.

Air audibly whooshed from her lungs. Her hair was dishevelled, and her mascara was smudged under her eyes as if she'd swiped away tears.

"My father has kept you both waiting a long time." Rashid forced sympathy into his tone, clamping down on his desire, anger, and confusion. His attention turned to the small dark-haired girl sitting at the table, headphones in her ears, mesmerised by a movie. His father was right. Sami looked like him. A lot like him. Too much like him for coincidence.

"Three hours," she snapped as she leaned over to pick up her bag. "Thank you for talking some sense into him. Your father is not my favourite person right now. Sami is four years old. How could he? I was terrified he'd incarcerate us or leave us in the desert to die and you'd think we were happily living in Australia. I was terrified for Sami."

His chest tightened and the urge to take her in his arms was beyond bearable, but he forced himself to stay still, to listen and to commiserate. "I'm sorry he put you through that."

"He had no right," she said with a stifled sob. "Thank you for coming to our rescue. Again. You *are* here to rescue us?" she asked, her fractured gaze colliding with his, cranking the tension inside him to new heights.

"Jemma, I apologise for my father's methods, but I can't apologise for the chance to see you again. To meet Sami." He studied the small girl who looked just like him. His heart twisted and ached. He'd left Jemma pregnant and alone? He wanted her in his arms, but she was colder than an arctic breeze. His heart felt like ballast in his chest. She stood expectantly with her bag slung over her shoulder.

"Your father is a bully."

"He comes from a different time, but I think you made your point."

"I did?" She stopped, shock apparent in her lifted brows, her eyes wide.

"He liked you."

"He did?"

"And so, too, does my mother."

"She does?" Her bravado deflated. "Then why are we being detained? Are we free to go now?" Her eyes shifted to the door.

"Yes," but he made no move to open it. His father's methods were archaic but effective. "I have something I need to say before you go." His gaze returned to hers. She took a visible breath and squared her shoulders. Her twisting hands belied the courage in her stance and his heart contracted.

"I know you feel betrayed," she burst out. "Which was never my intention. My focus was Aminah." Her cheeks flushed pink. "I should have realised how dangerous the book was for your family."

Rashid held his tongue. Kept the rising tide of excitement at bay. He would listen if it killed him, which it damn near did. She looked so beautiful and he had so much to say. It was all he could do not to pull her into his arms and take her mouth with his. Take. Demand. Feast. He reined it in. Leashed the hunger. The impatience. Tried to resist the gorgeous temptation. This was the woman he wanted for his wife. He had to play his hand carefully. Skilfully. This was important. Important for him. Important for Zahidah. And he planned to get it right.

He waited until she fell silent.

"I understand about the book. I know it was for Aminah. As a defensive strategy, it was inspired."

Jemma's eyes, liquid with unshed tears, held his and he wouldn't have broken the connection for all the water in the desert. He could see the myriad of feelings she sought to share. Attraction, yes. Apology too. Love? He wanted to think so, but fear cavorted with courage. He had to take the chance. Share his feelings. Open himself to the risk of rejection. He hadn't appreciated how fearful he was until this moment. She had the power to wound him—deeply. But this was a woman like no other. A woman who'd proven her loyalty to Aminah. It was a knowledge that settled the twisting panic in his gut. She was his equal. In every way and therein lay the difference.

"I was wrong." He lowered himself into the chair opposite Sami, but he kept his eyes on Jemma. She sank into the seat next to Sami and Rashid took her restless hands in his, soothing their fluttering movements with a sweep of his thumbs. Her hands looked pale and deceptively slight against the darker skin of his and he bolstered himself against the welling need to protect and defend.

"I know your freedom is important to you. From the beginning, you made it clear you stood alone and liked it that way. Your father wasn't available to you. You had no choice..." He squeezed her hands and waited. Her smile was brave, but he saw the vulnerability behind it. The fear, the uncertainty, the need. She deserved to be loved. Truly loved. *He loved her.* The truth was there. He loved her. He couldn't bear to live his life without her. He needed her and he just had to convince her she needed him.

"You had no choice. But now you do." He waited as confusion creased her brow, his attention drawn to the little girl beside her. Questions crowded his mind, but he pushed them back. "I'm not sure when, but I fell in love with you. I learned to respect you, to value your opinions and to enjoy your company. But more than that, I desire you. I love you. I think I always will. I thought it would be wrong to ask you to stay in Zahidah. I didn't want you to feel trapped here, but now I know, I should have allowed you to make that decision for yourself, for Sami.

I was wrong to make it for you. Marriage to me would be more binding than any other. You'd marry not only me, but my country and my people. You'd be bound in a way most people couldn't imagine. It wouldn't be easy for Sami either, but her well-being would be my priority. I want you to know before you leave that I love you. That I want you to be my wife. That I want you and Sami to stay in Zahidah. With me. But if you choose to leave, you go with my blessing. My heart is with you and always will be."

He paused, light-headed and giddy, as if his words had sucked the oxygen from the room. "I should have told you how I felt. Losing you was the hardest thing I've ever had to endure. Love is new to me. I didn't trust it. I thought…" Shut the hell up. He was speaking like an uncertain adolescent. He wished she'd say something. Her eyes poured with a torrent of tears. He passed her a wad of tissues and she blew her nose noisily. He yearned to take her in his arms and hold her there forever, but he hesitated. He didn't want her to think he was questioning her strength. Jemma needed no man to hold her up, but to stand by her side? Together?

"Say something. Please. I can't bear it. I don't know whether to take you in my arms or walk away and stop upsetting you. I need to know how you feel because I want you in my life forever. Not just for now." He was digging himself into a deeper hole. A dark space where fear suffocated him, sapping his breath and his strength. "Damn it, woman. Speak." Dignity was no longer an option. He'd laid his heart bare and if she didn't speak soon, he'd sink to her feet and beg.

"I love you, too…" she hiccoughed on a sob, "but there's something you should know and I don't expect you to feel the same way after I've told you and that's okay because I know you've been betrayed by women before and you'll think this is just further proof that women can't be trusted but it was for a good reason and I hope you'll hear me out, which is more than I deserve I know." She stopped to take a much-needed breath and her face looked stricken.

Hope surged through his veins like a tidal wave and for a long moment, he couldn't move, his limbs were snap frozen, his gaze fixed on hers. The energy that zapped between them was practically visible to the naked eye. She loved him. Elation and adrenaline shot through his veins, but that didn't mean she wouldn't leave. He was out of his seat within a moment, his pride no longer an option.

"Sami's my daughter, isn't she?" He had to ask. The question refused to be silenced. The words were out and between them before he'd had time to do more than grasp her hands between his.

She held his gaze with her watery one, her voice a whisper from parched lips. "Yes... I'm sorry... I..."

"I'm not sorry." He almost crushed her hands between his and his heart soared. "I'm thrilled, I'm blown away, and maybe I'm..."

"Pardon?" She looked more lost and vulnerable than he'd ever seen her.

"I'm sorry I wasn't there for you. I'm sorry you had to leave your husband, but I'm not sorry you left him. I'm relieved. Truly I am because I can't live without you or Sami." He stepped towards the smaller version of the woman he loved, so like her and so like him. Their daughter. The most precious gift imaginable.

"I lied to you. There was no husband. I didn't want you to feel obligated. I thought if I told you I was married... I'd never felt like that before and it scared me… I couldn't deal with it."

She was all his and his alone?

"I couldn't be happier to hear you lied to me. I should have told you I was promised to Fadila, but I didn't want to spoil what was the best night of my life and I didn't love her…"

"Neither one of us was able to commit back then. When I realised I was pregnant, and then discovered who you were, I thought it was best to stay out of your life, but then Sami got sick and we couldn't find a bone marrow match… she nearly died," Jemma whispered. "Aminah saved her. She was a perfect match. I owe Aminah everything. There is nothing I wouldn't do for her. Nothing."

"I understand now. You've been through so much," he soothed.

Jemma gently took the earbuds out of Sami's ears. "Honey, there's someone I'd like you to meet."

The little girl dragged her attention away from the screen.

Rashid knelt down to Sami's level. "Hi Sami," he stammered. "I'm Raz. What are you watching?"

"*Sleeping Beauty*. It's even better than Cinderella. Can we go now?"

"I'd really like it if you'd stay in Zahidah. If mummy agrees." He glanced up at the woman whose eyes spilled with love for their daughter. "I'm very excited to meet you. I know you've been sick, and you've been so brave. I'm so grateful you're going to be well."

"Mummy, why are you crying?" Sami asked, lifting her gaze to Jemma, who stood behind him, her eyes streaming.

"Because this is your daddy and I'm so happy for you to meet him," she said, the last word snagging in her throat and becoming a squeak. Rashid rose and took Jemma into his arms.

"I'm so happy you can finally meet her," she repeated, her voice muffled by the soft cotton of Rashid's shirt. She lifted her tear-washed gaze to his.

"Marry me," he urged. "If you can forgive me for leaving you alone to deal with all of this. My girls. So beautiful. I can't believe I nearly lost you both."

"I was so afraid you'd take Sami away from me... I couldn't bear to live without her. But I'm not my father and I would have had to..."

"You're the strongest woman I know, and I would never take Sami away from you. I can't wait to be a family. Together. You're not alone. Not anymore. We're a team. We're better together than we are apart. With you, I can make Zahidah better. With you, we can change things."

"Yes." She wept as she scooped Sami into a group hug. "What do you think, Sami? Shall mummy marry your daddy?"

"My daddy?" Sami breathed in awe. "And live happily ever after?"

"Yes," he promised. "In a palace and you'll be a princess. Would you like that?"

"Like Princess Aurora?" she whispered, her voice incredulous.

"Yes," he agreed. "And you'll get to meet your grandmother, the queen and your grandfather, the king."

"She's not an evil queen, is she?" Sami asked, her eyes rounding with concern.

"No, Sami, she's not," Jemma said with a smile. "She's brave and smart and beautiful, just like you."

Rashid held them both close as if to draw them into the very fabric of his soul. They belonged. With him. To protect and cherish and love from this day forward... until...

"Was that a yes, you'll both marry me?" he repeated, for he couldn't process it all quickly enough.

"Yes, we'll marry you," Jemma replied, her smile bursting through the watery mess of her tears. "But what about your father? He might not be happy with your choice of bride? Doesn't he like to do the choosing?"

"My mother was furious I'd allowed the *future queen of Zahidah* to leave without telling her how I felt. And my father wouldn't let you leave the country. Perhaps you're right. We can deal with them. I'm sure you're more than up to the task."

"Truly? She said that? He didn't want me to leave?"

"Yes and no." Rashid dragged them into a hug. With Jemma and Sami in his arms, he was the happiest man on earth. Home. He'd found it with Jemma. He hadn't known he was incomplete until she'd fitted against him like she was made to be there. Until he'd lost himself in her heady taste, her perfect body and found a peace he'd never known.

He pulled back, far enough to see into the turquoise magnificence of her eyes.

"My mother will be more than thrilled and Aminah will be beside herself with joy. She loves you both."

"We love her, too."

"I want to kiss you," he chided.

"Oh, I'm way ahead of you." They lowered Sami to the floor, and she ran about in excited delight. Jemma's lips were a nanosecond from his and when she closed the gap, his heart soared through the heavens like a runaway star.

This woman was his.

Princess Jemma bin Ra'ed Al Shahid. The mother of his child. His lover. His wife. And Sami. His precious daughter.

Epilogue

"Hurry, Raz. I don't want to be late." He looked amazing in a striking white robe, pristine and snowy against his deeply tanned skin. Freshly shaven and smelling so good she could have breathed his scent forever, Jemma leaned closer into his warmth. Evenings in Zahidah in November were cool, but Rashid radiated warmth and comfort. As his hand closed around hers, the tension in her muscles eased.

"We're an hour early. We're not going to be late," he soothed.

"It's Sami's first dressage competition. It's important she knows her parents are there to support her. Can you believe it? Our daughter can ride almost as well as her Auntie Aminah."

"Yes, she's incredible. Nearly as incredible as her beautiful mother." His steps slowed and he turned her towards him, engulfing her in an enormous hug. She couldn't stop the smile. Nor the feigned chagrin. "We'll be late."

"I thought we discussed that already. There's plenty of time to stop and take a breather." He rested his possessive hands over her swollen belly. She relaxed and allowed herself a moment of restorative pleasure.

Happiness fizzed in her veins. "I had roses delivered to the stables. Pink ones. I guess it's no surprise that Sami loves horses, given Aminah's love for them."

"I'm sure they'll be perfect and so are you."

"You're biased."

"I am and I can't wait to add another gorgeous girl to the fold, although I'm half afraid she'll inherit your temper." He paused, "I guess there's a chance she'll be demure like her grandmother."

"Your mother is all steely strength behind that persona."

"Yes, she is. I guess she recognised a kindred spirit in you."

Jemma thought of all they'd achieved in the past few years, advocating for Zahidan women, both within the monarchy and the community, satisfaction like syrup in her veins. Finally, she'd found her place. Her home. A place where she belonged and soon, soon... her mind shifted to the restive soul, so beloved, that was growing in her womb. Soon, she would welcome another daughter. Jordan. The thought was warmer than the sun. She couldn't wait to be a mother again.

Their child. Their baby. Jemma looked up at the wonderful man who was her husband.

"Thank you."

"For what?"

"For the family I've always wanted. I feel so blessed."

Joy radiated from inside. Happiness. Love. Family. She couldn't wait to meet her new daughter. To introduce her to Sami and her brother, Kareem.

"We are." Rashid's mouth covered hers and she sank into the heavenly bliss of his kiss. He tasted with passion and her body reacted like a fuse set to light. It was a long moment before Rashid pushed her back.

"Your Highness, we're on a public street," he murmured.

"So we are." Her voice was surprised. He'd sent her to paradise. A place where nothing existed except for Rashid.

A flash. She smiled as she realised the paparazzi had taken advantage of their distracted moment. Tomorrow, their kiss would be front-page news. Rashid linked his arm through hers and after a polite nod to the cameraman, they moved on towards the entrance to the arena.

"Do you think they'll ever get bored of it and stop traipsing after us?" he growled.

"No. Not when there's a new princess on the way." Jemma's smile stretched all the way to her toes.

"You're right. That's news the Zahidan people can't wait to hear." He wrapped his arm possessively around her and her heart soared.

"That's news I can't wait to share," said Jemma, her hand comforting the shifting child within as a small foot stretched and moved.

"You're beautiful."

"You just want another kiss." Joy swam in her veins. "I thought we were late."

"We have more than enough time," he promised, and spun her back into his arms.

"Forever's not long enough," she whispered into the velvet heat of his lips. Her heart swelled as her gaze connected with his. Dark eyes, filled with desire. "I love you, Raz."

"I love you, too, Your Highness. Always and forever." He kissed her on the nose and then on the forehead. "And soon we'll be five. I can't wait."

"Nor can I."

"Let's join the others. Kareem will be giving his Auntie Aminah the run around." Rashid pushed the door open and stepped aside to allow Jemma through. He joined her with a hand to the small of her back.

"I'm so excited I can hardly stand my nerves. Sami must be sick with them."

"Sami thrives on riding. It gives her such joy. I wish I could give her every horse in the kingdom."

"You're a generous man," she replied with a smile as he took her arm to support her.

"Facetious, Your Highness?"

"No. I mean it," she replied as she observed the arena, the perfectly manicured grass, luscious and green. Zahidah was a remarkable place and its new king was a remarkable man.

"It's lucky I've got you to guide me," he teased.

"It's lucky I've got you beside me," she said as he fielded the crowd.

"There's mother." He waved towards the older woman who was weaving her way towards them. Jemma's heart filled with joy. Nada was like the mother she'd never had. "And Aminah with Kareem."

Her life was complete. Family and love and joy beyond measure.

* * *

Thank you so much for reading *Desert Prince, Scandalous Affair!* I hope you enjoyed Jemma and Rashid's story.

Behind every great man is a great woman. And behind every great woman… is a great man! Jemma and Rashid are better together than they are apart, and I'm so glad that Sami has a big family to love her.

They say that the course of true love never did run smooth. This proverb comes from A Midsummer Night's Dream, by William Shakespeare. It is the difficulties that characters have to work through to find true love that make writing and reading romance fun.

If you enjoyed *Desert Prince, Scandalous Affair*, I'd really appreciate a review on your Amazon website of choice and/or on Goodreads: https://www.goodreads.com/book/show/41014887-desert-prince-scandalous-affair. Authors rely on readers' reviews to stand out (hopefully in a good way)!

And if you'd like to join my newsletter and receive a free welcome gift (Bachelor on Trial), I'd love to see you at: https://dl.bookfunnel.com/lzmhskru7g

You can also find me at www.lexigreene.com.au or on facebook at www.facebook.com/lexi.greene.75 or www.facebook.com/lovelexigreene.

Warmest regards,

Lexi Greene xx

About the Author

Lexi is an Australian author who loves to write powerful, passionate and provocative stories. She writes romance in the early morning and works as a paediatric neuropsychologist by day. A happily married mum of two teens, a parrot and a puppy, she loves to escape into a good story. She is a firm believer that a bath, a green tea and chocolate take a good book and make it perfect.

Lexi is a member of Romance Writers of Australia and Romance Writers of America; and is a huge fan of Margie Lawson's Writer's Academy.

Lexi loves a good happily ever after...

You can connect with me on:
f https://facebook.com/lexigreene.75

Subscribe to my newsletter:
✉ https://dl.bookfunnel.com/lzmhskru7g

Also by Lexi Greene

Bachelor on Trial
When Tony Radcliff joins Forbes lawyers, career-driven Scarlet O'Connor finds she has competition for the coveted partnership position.

And Tony has a couple of aces up his sleeve. Like his surf-sculpted body, which plays havoc with Scarlet's 'all work and no play' plans for partnership. And his brother, who holds the key to a secret from her past.

When Scarlet and Tony start steaming up the office windows, there's no doubt they're playing with fire. But there can only be one winner, so who gets burned?

https://bklnk.com/B08KLMJXQB

Bachelor on Board
Success is the best revenge.

Amber Reed, a rising television producer, needs her new show—Bachelor on Board, Australia—to outshine the one her ex stole from her, or risk losing her job to the conniving Lothario, but when her Bachelor falls in love and absconds with one of the contestants, she's forced to rely on Plan B, Nathan Moretti, the high school popular who broke her heart.

Nathan Moretti, soon-to-be head of the wealthy Moretti family, needs a wife to protect the family fortune from his gold-digger stepmother, and his job should be easy with twenty-four beautiful women to choose from. Right?

Not when the only woman he wants is the one behind the camera and her success relies on him finding love with someone else, on screen, on schedule, as promised. Can Amber forgive the past and risk her heart—again?

https://bklnk.com/B08KPFWW7D

Once Upon a Christmas Wish

Jenn Adams is determined to tick off her bucket list and face her past nemeses—learning to ski and a man named Brad.

Brad Oregon is the only man she's ever loved. His chocolate eyes. His to-die-for smile. His toned body. His very toned body.

But Brad's reputation with women is almost as renowned as his ski-racing success. Now a ski instructor in beautiful Whistler, he's as difficult to resist as the scenery! What the hell. Life is short. A two-week holiday romance should suit them both perfectly. Right?

https://bklnk.com/B07LBM48NN

Shatterproof

Emily Stone, an internationally successful model on the brink of supermodel stardom, appears to have it all. All, except love, because Emily wants the kind of man who isn't fooled by the pretty. She wants the kind of love that's big enough and true enough to include her disabled sister and dysfunctional mother.

Nick was an A-list actor in tinsel town with a super-sized ego until a tragic car accident stole his wife, his unborn child, and his gilded career, leaving him physically and emotionally scarred.

When wintry French Island brings these two wayward souls home, shared childhood memories aren't enough to bridge the deep divide forged by their adult lives and choices.

That is until Carmie, Emily's delightful Down Syndrome sister, weaves her special kind of magic. Can Carmie's boundless love and infectious joy help them to heal their broken hearts or will the glamour of Emily's work-world whisk her away?

https://bklnk.com/B07YTN294C